Nocturne Variations

John Biscello

Published by Unsolicited Press

www.unsolicitedpress.com

info@unsolicitedpress.com

Copyright © 2018 John Biscello

All Rights Reserved.

Unsolicited Press Books are distributed by Ingram.

Printed in the United States of America.

Attention schools and businesses: for discounted copies on large orders, please contact the publisher directly.

Cover Design: Heather Ross

Editor: S.R. Stewart; Kristen Gustafson

ISBN: 978-1-947021-66-2

Nocturne Variations

John Biscello

Notes on Lighting:

If you leave a print or photograph out in the light too long, the image will eventually disappear. Light, in this respect, is a double-edged sword. Exposure and the fade of exposure, in equal measures.

Light is also a traitor, an enigma, a crisis, and an outlet for grief.

Production Notes:

Let us begin in storied darkness and go from there.

It is important to mention that in this production, God, having strayed from his original vocation, has become a cinefile with short-term memory loss. He wields a camera like an insomniac with nostalgia for scrim.

His omniscient eye wanders. Constantly. Never settling on one thing for too long.

High-bottom A.D.D. to the nth degree.

Here, there, everywhere—typhoid Mary, the proverbial rhyme in a nursery school sermon.

Technical Notes:

Deep focus, in film, as in the depth of the shot. Creating dimensional layers.

What about deep focus when the camera points toward the interior?

How to shoot a deep focus of the interior life—how one incident is connected to another, a complex geography of moods and emotions, a trigger-sensitive interplay?

"You will see that this little clicking contraption with the revolving handle will make a revolution in our life—in the life of writers. It is a direct attack on the old methods of literary art. We shall have to adapt ourselves to the shadowy screen, and to the cold machine. A new form of writing will be necessary. I have thought of that and I can feel what is coming. But I rather like it. This soft change of scene, this blending of emotion and experience—it is much better than the heavy, long-drawn-out kind of writing to which we are accustomed. It is closer to life. In life, too, changes and transitions flash before our eyes, and emotions of the soul are like a hurricane. The cinema has divined the mystery of motion. And that is greatness."

—Leo Tolstoy, on his eightieth birthday, 1908

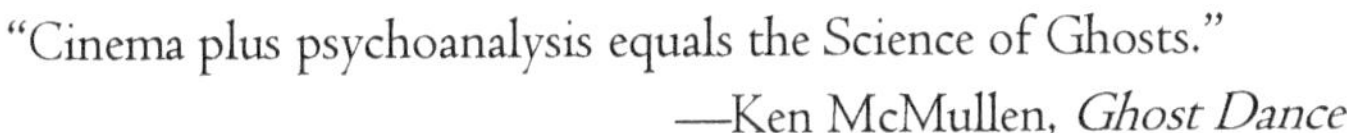

"Cinema plus psychoanalysis equals the Science of Ghosts."
—Ken McMullen, *Ghost Dance*

It is like closing your eyes and trying to connect the dots.

This is what Piers is thinking as she sculpts fire onto the blondegirl's breasts.

Her hands work over the cotton-knit sweater, and then under, fingers skimming bra as if it were runway Braille.

Piers and the blondegirl, whose name is Tracy, are at Tabanid, a nightclub on Sunset. Specifically, Piers and Tracy are in the coat-nook, a place where Piers often takes the girls she meets at the club.

Piers and Tracy's mouths are grafted together in animal wedlock,

their tongues like forked lightning, flashing pearls of saliva.

Because Piers, at 5'2", is shorter than Tracy, 5'7", there is a furious incline to her kissing, to her desire.

Outside the coat-nook, a rapping on the door followed by a voice—Piers. Fucking Piers. It's time to go on. Get yer ass out here. PIERS.

The voice belongs to Trink, Piers's shadow-show partner.

Piers disengages her mouth from Tracy's.

The two girls are panting, inflamed.

Piers steps back, allowing her perspective to widen.

Tracy tucks stray bits of hair behind her ear.

Piers can't tell if Tracy's eyes are blue or green. She asks.

They change depending on the light, Tracy responds with obvious pride in this quality.

They change according to the light, Piers repeats, smiling, relishing the prickly sensation just below her navel.

Piers draws nearer to Tracy, isolating her perspective to Tracy's face.

(Trink: Put your tongue back in your mouth and get yer ass out here.)

You're so fucking beautiful, Piers smooths her hand over Tracy's cheek.

Tracy, in turn, runs her fingers over Piers's fuzz-coated scalp—I like your shaved head. The way it feels. And I like your tongue piercing.

Piers sticks out her tongue and wags it, modeling the ribbed silver stud bobbing on pink.

Then she springs forward, tongue lancing Tracy's sealed lips.

Again, the kissing, the groping, connecting the dots.

(Trink: I'm leaving Piers. You hear me? Bye!)

Piers withdraws—Guess I gotta go.

Then, clutching a swath of coat, Piers asks Tracy—Do you like leather?

What do you mean?

Piers takes a blue leather raincoat off its hanger and places it like a shawl over Tracy's shoulders.

Who does it belong to, Tracy asks.

I don't know. Maybe a lady named Suzanne.

Huh?

Never mind. It's yours.

I can't just—

Ssssshhhh (index pinning Tracy's lips) it's impolite to refuse a gift. See you after the show.

Wait, one more thing.

Piers tears the sleeve of the raincoat.

There. Now it's perfect.

Outside, a screen of white linen, attached to two wooden poles separated by about nine feet.

An industrial floor lamp, and a series of overhead lights are switched on, illuminating the screen from different angles.

Behind the screen, to the left, Trink is already set up. He is standing next to the chair he will sit in during the performance. Set on the stage, in front of the chair: Fisher-Price xylophone, acoustic guitar, djembe, and gourd rattle. There is a Gatorade bottled filled with vodka and pink lemonade, a bright pink straw sticking out of the bottle.

When Piers finally arrives on stage, behind the screen, her shadow appears to the audience, who may or may not hear the following exchange between her and Trink.

You and your bitches in the closet Piers. Fucking boil and hiss.

It's a nook, Trink. Not a closet. A nook.

Fuck nook. It's bullshit is what it is.

Mind your business is what it is.

This *is* my business. Yours too. We're here to put on a show, ain't we?

Piers doesn't respond as she goes through her trunk, taking out the shadow puppets she will need for the show.

They've already announced us ya know?

For some reason this statement amuses Piers, makes her smile. Shadow puppets laid out in their proper order, Piers walks over to Trink, pinches then tugs on his left earlobe.

You're the best Trink, you know that? The very, very best. I love you.

Trink turns his head, wanting to hide the lighted slash that has displaced his scowl.

You and your charms. Little fucking foxfire aintcha? (pause, exhale) Okay, ready to conjure some magic?

Piers responds by making her fingers dance.

Trink steps out from behind the screen, and the audience's

view of what had been a silhouette morphs into a svelte black man, cased in a shiny purple corset, tight black velvet bellbottoms, glitter-encrusted platforms, and a harmonic blitz of make-up, mostly emphasizing silver.

Ladies and gentlemen and unclassifieds
(ripples of audience laughter)
As some of you already know
I go by the name Trink
and my partner back there hiding behind the screen
(the audience sees the silhouette of a giant hand waving)
goes by the name Piers.
We specialize in shadow shows
and tonight's presentation has to do with
those age-old friends and enemies
(dramatic pause)
Cock and Pussy. Not to be confused with Punch and Judy.
(laughter, a few whistles, scattered applause)
For you old-old-schoolers who might be up to speed on your Greek theater
our show was inspired by Aristophane's classic battle of the sexes Lysistrata.
Our shady remix titled 'Straddling Lizzy'
raises the important question: Can pussy no more
put an end to male-ordered wars?
(riotous applause)
Trink bows his head and disappears behind the screen.

Straddling Lizzy, shadow play performed at Tabanid, December 14th, 1989

Audience perspective:

We are staring at a blank white screen.

Slowly the filtration of shell-pink light spreads like infant-rash over white.

Along the edges of the roseate aura, traces of turquoise and green.

Morning.

The hoarse crowing of a rooster. Brutal, insistent.

A bed, in sharp profile, appears at the base of the screen.

A serene guitar melody, kinked with Latin accents, begins playing

as the blanket, perched on what looks like a pole, rises off the bed

and keeps rising.

When the blanket reaches the top of the screen

the pole, in sync with the melody stops.

Silence, stillness.

A Xylophonic groove, like nursery school disco, kicks in, and letters, vivid and funky-fresh, splash onto the screen, one by one by one until we can read:

S
  t
   r
    a
     d
     d
      l
       i
        n
         g
           Lizzy?

Behind the screen, Trink:

From where Trink is sitting he sees Piers at an angle, mostly from behind. Piers, engaged in a rhapsody, in the throes of a manual dervish, and at times Trink swears that she grows a second and third hand, or a tentacle or something, in manipulating her cut-outs.

Trink first saw Piers on the Venice Beach boardwalk, performing a shadow play version of Aesop's "The Lion and the Mouse" (except in Piers's version, the Mouse operated more like a fox, using cunning and guile to make the Lion its slave) and was mesmerized by the virtuosity displayed by the raggedy street urchin with big eyes. That was how Trink initially thought of Piers.

Trink finishes an atonal melody on his xylophone (underscoring the dire rumor which has just reached Bruno and the other men: the women are talking about going on a sex-strike until the men give up warring) and picks up his Gatorade bottle, sipping from the straw.

He stares out at Piers, an imp having a seizure.

This is when Trink loves her the most. When she is slotted between worlds, neither here nor there, flickering, amorphous.

Trink sets down the Gatorade bottle, squeezes the djembe between his thighs, and waits his cue before beating out a tribal rhythm.

Behind the screen, Piers:

Within her frame of vision float miniature men and women peopled with ghosts. Their intent is to punish and love one another, to commit arson. The purpose of their actions matter significantly less to Piers than their movements, the dancing of their actions, the concert of their relationship, i.e., how Lizzy swivels her palm, a subtle yet powerful gesture that causes Bruno

to collapse inward, crumpling at the waist and knees, until he has become a small boy cowed at the feet of his mother.

Piers can feel the psychology behind their movements, can feel isolated parts struggling for unity.

In this world there is no Trink, no audience, no Piers,

just a series of modulating impressions wholly dependent upon light and shadow.

"When Alexander von Bernus says of the shadow play that it reflects 'in its purest form the dematerialized world of waking dreams,' he has in mind the magic area where the threshold between this world and the next world is crossed by ghosts and demons."

–Günter Böhmer, *The Wonderful World of Puppets*

The show has ended and we are now in the upstairs room at Tabanid, the room known as the Attic. It is sort of a private clubhouse, a vice den with no regard for the future.

You will notice that just about everyone in the room, nearly a dozen, are holding cloths which they intermittently raise to their faces, covering their mouths and nostrils to inhale, as if chloroforming themselves. This is known as huffing Sike.

Sike, short for Cycle-All, is an experimental chemical compound, a clear liquid, that is poured in trace amounts onto a cloth. Typically, a user has their signature cloth, the one they employ repeatedly, developing and deepening a bond between chemical, cloth, and user. Some euphemistically refer to this as the Unholy Trinity. Others call it Three and Out.

Trink initiated Piers into the world of Sike about nine months ago.

He had pulled her aside at a party, and in a reverential hush told her how Sike was the closest thing to Childhood he had ever experienced.

Piers, who was no stranger to narcotics and the places they led, asked Trink—Is it *like* Childhood, or is it Childhood, you know its own incarnation?

At first Trink was puzzled by Piers's question, then caught a handle—It's more Childhood than Childhood. Better than the real thing. It's like, you know, when they say, have you ever heard them say how you can paint an apple and make it more apple than the real apple? The appleness of apples, the essence.

The appleness of apples. This concept had stuck with Piers, grew claws, dug in deep, not to mention the quality of Trink's voice when talking about Sike, warm and sad and sweetly reverent.

The first time Piers had huffed Sike she heard an undeveloped cry, an under ripe moaning. It was both near and far. That was when she realized there was very little metaphysical distance (or difference) between her wailing *like* a five-year-old, and her *as* a wailing five-year-old. What she later wrote in her journal: Chronology is a fiction and parallelism a fact.

The second time Piers huffed Sike she wondered—If Childhood is a continuum and a repository for lost things, might she be able to find her mother there, and perhaps, claim a piece of her, a necessary and vital shard?

There is a movie projector situated more or less in the center of the room. The film being projected onto the white wall is *Scarlet Street*, a 1945 noir film, directed by Fritz Lang and starring Edward G. Robinson.

The tall man with the boxy countenance, wearing a snakeskin coat (python from Africa) and brown leather cowboy hat (Australian bush) staring at the flickering black-and-white images, is called DeLeon. He is the owner of Tabanid, and the man from whom everyone buys Sike. DeLeon doesn't huff Sike, nor does he drink or smoke or indulge in chemical substances. DeLeon is cine-maniacal, movies are his vice and passion. He doesn't just watch films but consults them the way one might consult the Tarot or I-Ching. If he needs to make a major decision, if he's seeking guidance or direction, he refers to film.

DeLeon has shot a number of film shorts and screen tests. These were not intended for screening or distribution but rather for his personal collection. He was aware that they lacked any real merit or entertainment value. He simply enjoyed shooting and watching them. For a number of years, DeLeon has also been trying to write a screenplay. He has never gotten more than thirty to forty pages in before he scraps what he's written and starts again, after a period of repose. The latest incarnation of the screenplay is titled *Midnight Over Noon*. Its bloodline is noir.

In surveying the Attic of the Tabanid, we see white faux-leopard couches lining two of the walls, a half-dozen wooden chairs, and two tall metal tables with stools attached. The novelty of the stools is that they rotate around the table at different speeds (a dial, located on the underside of the table, is how you regulate the speeds). Bleary rashes of soft red emanate from the Chinese lanterns hanging from the ceiling which, aside from the movie projector, are the only sources of light in the room. In the middle of the floor, just behind the projector, there is a white bear-cloud of a throw rug, which is where Piers and Tracy are sitting, cross-legged, Tracy still wearing the blue raincoat that Piers stole earlier.

Piers's forehead is braced against Tracy's. Her fingers touch at the torn sleeve of the raincoat, its texture glossy and mesmeric. Her other hand is clutching her signature cloth, which is baby blue.

Piers fevers her tongue inside Tracy's mouth and grows happy and woozy and lost. Then an edge creeps in, a spiked alert, to which Piers immediately responds by pulling away from Tracy, pouring a measured amount of Sike from the umber vial set by her side onto her cloth and then placing the cloth over her mouth and nostrils to inhale tainted renegade oxygen.

Piers, after each spell of huffing, will offer the cloth to Tracy, who each time will say thanks but no thanks, I'll stick with alcohol and weed.

Piers will nod and, eyes closed, fall back into kissing Tracy,

the felt bluish burn registering Tracy's entire body

as a memory in chrysalis, a slow becoming, and unravel.

Between kissing and petting and Piers's huffing, there was talk. Mostly it was Tracy telling Piers how amazing the show was, how talented Piers is, and Piers deflecting the praise and turning it back on Tracy—how beautiful you are, where have you been all my life, let's spend the night together, stuff like that.

Sometime later, Piers is stalled by a bad feeling.

What is it, Tracy asks, sensing the change.

Piers feels the bad in her stomach, a cold cramped fist, and is unsure why until she looks up and sees DeLeon and Trink in the far corner of the room, partly illuminated by ghostlight spilling over from the projector.

Trinks' posture, and the way in which DeLeon is moving his hand indicates tension, a breach of harmony.

Piers rises to stand,

(Tracy: Where you going?)

walks toward Trink and DeLeon,

(Tracy: Piers Piers what's going on?)

and chooses a spot against the wall, where she pretends to be watching the movie.

She listens, but Trink and DeLeon are done talking, and when DeLeon places his hand on Trink's shoulder, Piers's breathing grows animal and irregular,

and she thinks how breakable Trink is,

how very much like beautiful glass,

and her throat tightens considerably.

Only when DeLeon has removed his hand from Trink's shoulder and Trink walks away does the sense of menace dissipate.

Trink, crossing the room, doesn't notice Piers—

Hey, Piers grabs at Trink's arm.

Hey babygirl, where you coming from? You coming from fun?

Trink smiles big and his mascara-popped eyes set on Piers, obliquely.

Yea-yea. Coming from fun. Everything cool between you and DeLeon?

Oh yea, everything's fine. Just having one of our man-to-fag talks, ya know

Yea, but which one is which—

You quick on the draw Peersy. Start calling you Peersy-the-

Kid. The Keeed (short laugh) Hey, a funny thing, after the show I talked to that lady, what's her name, that lady who's gonna do the review in L.A. Piques. Anyways she was asking me about you—cuz, Bitch, *you* didn't talk to her, Miss Reluctant Artist and shit—so she's asking me a buncha questions and we get into the theme and content of Lysistrata, how it's often seen through a political and feminist prism and all that jazz, and you know what I said—

What?

I said, Piers just likes dick jokes.

Piers and Trink laugh and Piers calls Trink a bitch and Trink high-fives his agreement and Piers's bad feeling melts away entirely and stays gone even when she finds out that Tracy has left.

Piers and Trink freshen their cloths and huff and then go downstairs to dance.

In the Shadow of Abstinence and War

by Alistair Borden

Its incarnations have been varied—ballet, opera, comic-strip, movie musical western (the 1956 film, *The Second Anarchist Sex)—*and we can now add shadow puppetry to the list of disciplines that have resurrected the old bones of Aristophane's *Lysistrata*.

Originally performed in classical Athens, 411 B.C., *Lysistrata's* satirical spindrift revolves around women locking their legs and withholding sex from men until they put an end to the Peloponnesian War. In what becomes the ultimate battle of the sexes, the speculative gauntlet is thrown: Will the women put out before the men give in?

Leaping millennia ahead to the date December 14, 1989, a.k.a. last Thursday, on which *Lysistrata's* contemporary shadow-double *Straddling Lizzy* was performed at Tabanid. I confess to having seen only a handful of shadow shows in my life and might have missed out on this wonderful piece if not for the urging of my friend, David, a puppeteer and lover of classical Greek anything.

Prior to attending the show, David schooled me on the history shadow theater, with its ambiguous origins potentially dating as far back as second century B.C. in India. Yet the popular legend of its "beginnings" can be traced back to 120 B.C., during the Han Dynasty in China. As the legend goes, the Emperor Wu-Ti was grieving the death of his favorite wife, Wang, and was desperate to see her again. Enter a gentleman named Sciao-wong, who said he could make Wang appear again, and did so, night after night, a silhouette floating behind a white screen. In respecting Sciao-wong's magic, the Emperor was instructed to not look behind the screen and honored this request, until one night curiosity got the best of him. Similar to how Dorothy would shockingly discover thousands of years later in a different faraway land, the Emperor discovered that the Wizard was no Wizard at all but rather a man conjuring illusions.

Allegedly, Sciao-wong's story ended in one of two ways: 1. He was decapitated for deceiving the Emperor. 2. He was granted a special title and fortune and ordered to keep making Wang appear nightly.

Throughout the ages in different cultures, specifically Eastern ones, shadow shows have functioned as exorcisms, séances, religious celebrations, and marathon homages to myths and epics. Yet, on the more transgressive side, they have also served as satirical mouthpieces, delivering thinly veiled barbs and digs against the powers that be (in Egypt, around the middle of the 15th century, the sultan Tsachaknak, in the name of orthodoxy, ordered all the shadow figures to be burned). In this respect, *Lysistrata* and shadow theater are ideal bedfellows.

Straddling Lizzy opens with an abstracted beanstalk erection, and from there the show grows into a freewheeling yet technically controlled farce of light and shadow. The Peloponnesian War has been replaced by the Phalliproscenium War and Lizzy, the lead character, is unlike her predecessor Lysistrata in that she is not a widow, but is married to a soldier named Bruno. During the course of the show, we come to learn that Bruno, Hemingway-esque in his pomp and bravura, enjoys anal sex (giving), fellatio (receiving), guns, television, and magical ponies (this being his big secret, which we find out during a hilarious monologue/song called "*All Ponies Prance in Heaven*").

Like the Emperor Wu-Ti and Dorothy before me, I wondered about the wizard in the shadows and discovered that a twenty-one-year old female, Piers, was the virtuoso behind the sorcery. After the show I got to meet the "wizard" who, with her cleanly shaved head, gleaming saucer eyes and waifish frame, reminded me of Sinead O' Connor's elfin sibling.

All of the show's music, which was quite eclectic in its range of styles, was performed by the twenty-five-year-old Trink, who meritoriously shifted between guitar, percussion, gourd, and Fisher-Price xylophone (an instrument that Trink has been playing since he was five). Trink's piercing falsetto on the haunting dirge "*Funeral Wrongs & Rites*" brought a collective hush to the audience while his beatboxing skills provided the piston-powered underlay to the rap-battle scene between the men and women, a.k.a. "*Libertease & Bustesses*". And, in the case of Augie, a sausage merchant who begins selling ribbed dildos to the women (and the

men), Trink offers a punk-klezmer send-up of
"If I Were a Rich Man" titled *"All the Wars
Make Rich Men"*.

Straddling Lizzy is chock full of verbal
punnilinguis and barbed innuendo, with many
of the verses metered to a sort of Seussian,
hip-hop swing. The following are bite-sized
samples of the rhythmical fare:

Lizzy (addressing Bruno):
Lizzy the Muse
has gone on vacation
stationed in her place
is a Bitch with a whip
on her boobs, you may say tits
with a grudge to bear bluntly,
or dub me a cunt, Cuneiform for queen-
lovely,
but lustlove you these tits
no more to be suckled
or snickered or buggered
or gobbled or badgered.

Bruno's bright idea, addressing the men:
I've got it me droogs
an orgy with ho's
Caligula's Roast
we'll name it and toast
our weenies to warm
in vaginal stoves

(When Bruno's plan to satiate the men's
needs through prostitutes goes bust, some of

the men, in secret, begin to bugger each
other and sexual orientation crises becomes
a sub-plot.)

And Lizzy, after having tease-tortured
Bruno by walking around the house in a
negligee:
   I am going to meet
   my negligee-encoded
   Dionysian posse
   of pussy-withholding sisters,
   picture us all
   parading around the square,
   scented, shapely,
   and clit-achely wondering:
   when o when will men
   give up their guns
   for really. . . good. . . head.

Though the word play, at times, can be a
bit of a lyrical overkill, perhaps due to a
self-aware affection for its own cleverness,
that is also part of where its rogue charms
lie. Musicality, verve, and Joie de vivre is
at the mischievous heart of it all, but its
ultimate magic lies in the puppets.
   Piers manipulates them with grace and
dexterous precision, and at times you'd
swear there was the multi-limbed sorcery of
Shiva at work. One style of puppet, created
exclusively for this show, were Hydras, a
cubistic conglomeration of faces and limbs
controlled by a tri-pronged rod. While
Lizzy, Bruno, and several others, are

individuated puppets, the "women" and the "men" are Hydras, allowing different characters and voices to be expressed through a single puppet. The "chorus" was also a Hydra, looking very much like a Can-Can troupe as imagined by Hieronymus Bosch.

In a year which has seen President Bush proclaim his agenda-driven "War on Drugs", Oliver North indicted for his involvement in the Iran-Contra scandal, and tensions between the U.S. and a Noriega-led Panama reach a boiling point, war, unfortunately, remains a relevant catchword and contagion. In this respect, Aristophane's satire remains a sharp and resonant echo among the world of shadows.

Straddling Lizzy will next be performed on New Year's Eve, when Tabanid hosts their burlesque-fashion show, Winter's Brides. Tickets, which include a champagne toast at midnight, are $35, and can be purchased in advance. 21/over. Tabanid is located at 8874 Sunset Blvd, (310) 358-1741.

"On the other hand, coming back to the Wu-Ti legend, the story corresponds in every way to what the shadow show meant at its religious origins: an evocation of the dead. The shadows were originally spirits recalled by evocators, or remembrances of the dead. These spirits were represented by figures artistically cut out from paper or leather and seen in profile on the screen. For this reason, the screen, the stretched cloth that separates the viewer from the figure and from those who make it move, is called in China 'Screen of Death.' In Java it is called 'Fog and Clouds'; in Turkey, 'Curtain of the Departing (of the hour of death); in Arabia, 'Screen of Dreams, Veil of the Omnipotent Secret.' With the shadow show we find ourselves in the area where shadows, dreams, and death meet. In many countries the shadow is equated with death, and this kind of show is, as no other, a secret spell, magic."

—René Simmen, The World of Puppets

Look, mommy, that man has an eye patch, like a pirate.

The young girl pointed out the car window at the man rounding up stray shopping carts.

Yes, the mother agreed without looking, instead surveying the parking lot for an open space.

The man, after having shoved a cart into the compacted line of carts, got the mother's attention by holding up his hand.

The mother slowed down the car.

The man gestured to where a spot was opening up.

The mother waved her thank you, allowed her car to idle, and then pulled in after the other car had pulled out.

The pirate helped us Mommy, the daughter beamed.

Yes, he did, the mother agreed. I guess he's a good pirate.

The daughter, who had just watched a movie adaptation of *Treasure Island*, considered the man more closely. Eye patch aside, he wasn't exactly dressed like a pirate. Winter hat, coat, gloves, jeans, boots. Pretty much how normal people dressed.

Mommy do you *really* think that man's a pirate, the daughter asked as they got out of the car.

I don't think so, honey. Put your hood on, it's cold. Give me your hand.

The daughter snugged her hood over her head and took her mother's hand.

Why not, she asked as they walked toward the store.

Because pirates usually don't work at Wal-Mart, was what almost flew out of the mother's mouth, but something — warmed-over residue of what it was like to have been a child— stopped her and instead she said—Because pirates usually hang out on their ships.

She looked down at her daughter, who looked up at her, nodding.

Oh yea, the daughter said, as if it were some fact that she had forgotten, and she wanted to go back and ask the pirate why he wasn't on his ship, but then she was inside the store, which was decked out for the holidays, and thoughts of the pirate were displaced by thoughts of Santa Claus.

The man, Henry Hook, helped several other drivers to find parking spots. After directing one lady, he heard—You the parking lot angel?

He turned around and saw that it was Hector, his co-worker, walking towards him.

Hector was blowing into cupped hands.

It's cold as balls out here, Hector announced, then went back to blowing.

Henry didn't understand a lot of Hector's phrases (why were balls cold?) but he enjoyed them all the same.

You need a pair of gloves, Henry told him.

I got some, just didn't bring 'em. Can I bum a smoke Henry?

Henry took off a glove, withdrew a pack of Winstons from his coat-pocket, and held it out to Hector, who wheedled a cigarette from the pack and tucked it behind his ear.

Muchas gracias, amigo.

Henry nodded, asked—How is it in there?

Oh man, it's a fucking madhouse. The whole store is bi-polar. People laughing and smiling, people growling and looking like they wanna murder someone. It's nuts. What time does your shift end?

Henry scanned his wrist-watch.

About twenty minutes.

Nice, Hector approved, then cleared his throat and spit. He began rocking on his heels, as if a song had just started playing in his head.

Henry, from the periphery of his good eye, noticed a car crawling along, in search of a space.

He signaled to the driver, indicating a spot where someone was about to pull out.

Hector laughed sharply—Look at you, Wallyworld's own holiday fucking valet. They should be paying you extra.

Henry smiled.

Hector spit again.

All right man, gonna head to the side of the store and smoke this stogie before my break's over. You working tomorrow?

No, I'm off. You?

Yea. Well, have yourself a happy Christmas.

You too, Hector. Here, a present—

Henry shook a cigarette from the pack and handed it to Hector.

Hector placed the cigarette between his lips and thanked Henry.

Henry watched as Hector sprinted across the parking lot, weaving between cars. Then he shifted his gaze to the far end of the parking lot.

The streetlamps had turned on.

The winter light was slowly bruising to dark.

Henry looked up at the sky. He figured it would snow. First snow of the year, which was coming later than usual.

First snow of the year always summoned the memory of the blizzard of '45, when the entire town was frosted in tiers of white. He was nine at the time, and he and his friend, Jake, had made money shoveling driveways. There were also the epic snowball fights, the building of snow-forts, and the hours that were spent sledding down Griffin Hill, where it seemed every kid in town was sledding.

An oil painting depicting the sledding spree at Griffin Hill hung at Red's. It was painted by a local artist, Gustav Brynner, who was now dead.

Henry, for the first time, wondered if the painting was for sale, and if so, how much did it cost? Maybe he would ask Gwen when he got to Red's, which was where he'd be going as soon as he got off work.

They were spinning slowly, ever so slowly.

Do you want to go faster, Piers reached down for the dial. I can make us go faster.

No, Anya smiled. I like the speed. We're moving so slow it's like we're not moving at all.

Piers and Anya sat in the Amusement Seats, across from one another.

Piers drew the cloth to her face, huffed, then passed it to Anya.

Piers stared at Anya, half her face masked in cloth, an asthmatic bandit in the throes of huffing.

Piers stared and stared,

and her vision dissimulated into small birds,

winging across the painted winter of Anya's face,

and into the rabbitpink of her eyes, a dying sun

or lighted prehistory.

And then, like a slow-motion dream in reverse,

Piers found herself earlier in the night:

Anya, on stage, a glacial Venus, dancing with the other Winter's Brides,

dancing to invoke snow, which came in the form of electro audio fuzz.

Can you hear the snow falling, Piers elated to Trink,

who nodded—Yea, yea, I can hear it babygirl, I can hear it.

The Brides, rejoicing in prayer, intensified the frenzy of their dancing,

as the snowfalling amped into a blizzard of white noise,

that raged and raged and then

Silence.

A ribbed, cathedral silence,

freezing the Brides into a penitent tableau.

And then, the frizzy feel of cloth in hand, returning Piers to Anya who was now sitting across from her, Anya has handed me the cloth and I have just huffed, and I am now saying to Anya—Remember when you were a kid and you'd spin and spin and spin as fast as you could until you fell down and it was like the greatest thing in the world? Did you do that?

Anya laughed—Yes, I did that. I think kids everywhere do that, no matter where they grew up.

Where did you grow up?

In the Ukraine. In a small village. Where did you grow up?

I didn't.

Piers laughed, as did Anya.

No, I grew up in South Dakota. In this town called Belle Fourche.

Belle Fourche, ah. What does Belle Fourche mean?

It means 'Beautiful Fork'. Not for me though. It was more like 'Ugly Knife Twisting in My Side'. How was it growing up in a small village and being different?

Different? Because I'm albino?

Yes.

It was sometimes hard. People could be cruel. But I learned how to tune out the negative stuff.

Now you're a beautiful ice fairy in L.A. you are made of ice and snow and magic, you know that, right?

Yes, Anya played along, and even though it's past midnight I haven't melted yet, the spell hasn't worn off. I get to be an ice fairy for a little while longer, and then—

And then?

And then I don't know.

Anya laughed.

Piers placed her hand over Anya's.

Anya's hand is warm. She is an ice fairy with warm hands, Piers thought.

Anya stared at the small pink offering astride her hand and said nothing.

It was almost two hours into the new year, and the new decade.

Piers and Trink opened the evening with *Straddling Lizzy*, which had been followed by *Winter's Brides*. The show comprised albino-only performers. DeLeon, himself albino, had imagined transforming Tabanid into a winter's dream, which is exactly what he had done. An ice sculpture of Botticelli's Venus had been the centerpiece of the refashioned setting.

Anya, like the other performers, was made of white and blue and pink. All other tones and colors had been abolished, a calculated extinction in composing a Winter's Bride.

How do you feel, Piers squeezed Anya's hand.

I feel fucking amazing. Anya scrunched her bare shoulders toward her ears. I feel like that little girl who spins around and around and falls down and is happy. I feel just like her.

You *are* her.

I am?

Yes. Deep, deep in your eyes. I can see it. I can see her. Or maybe her ghost.

Anya's lighted face dimmed to solemn. She bowed her head and began to cry.

Piers expected that the tears of an ice fairy would instantly freeze, but they didn't. They filigreed silver, like slash-marks in snow.

Piers kissed the back of Anya's hand, and then her wrist. She feathered her lips against the ridges of Anya's knuckles.

Trink, in full gale mode, blasted in.

He placed one hand on Anya's shoulder, one on the back of Piers's head, and intoned a benediction—I hereby absolve thee of all sins accumulated in the year previous. You are free to sin anew and may your Innocence multiply at the speed of first and last kisses.

Trink withdrew his hands from Piers and Anya—I shoulda been a priest, huh?

Anya laughed and wiped at her tears with the back of her hand.

Piers lifted her head and turned to Trink, who was staring at Anya.

You crying sweetheart? Trink gentled his fingers through Anya's frosted hair. What did Piers do to you?

Piers didn't do anything, Anya said. It's just, I remembered something, and then I started crying.

Ain't that always the way, Trink maternally cradled Anya's head.

When it comes to memories, Trink continued, there ain't no bigger crybaby than yours truly. As for our little Peersy here, she ain't much of a crier. I think all her tears go into her puppets. They do all her crying for her. Show us your hands.

Piers, smiling, displayed her hands, palms down.

The other side, Trink asserted.

Piers flipped her hands, palms up.

See right here, Trink traced several lines etched into Piers's palm. If you look real closely you'll notice that these lines got a bluish tinge. That's from the tears she cries through her hands. When her hands start weeping she closes 'em like this—

Trink folded Piers's fingers and thumb inward

—And she sends the tears back. She banishes them like bad kittens, like. . . you ever see a river reverse its course? Ever see it run backwards?

No, Anya said, I don't think so—

Well the river runs backwards in the case of our curious

specimen Pierangela—

Pierangela's your real name, that's beautiful—

Thanks—

And Pierangela's backward river of tears becomes a shadow show, right, Pierangela—

Right, Trink—

You two are funny—

Then come to the beach with us—

The beach—

Yea, that's why I came over, a bunch of us, including your Winter's Bridesmates, are gonna go to the beach and keep the party going till the sun comes up—

And then what happens, we melt—

Yea, you and the ice fairies melt, and me and Trink, we. . . what happens to us Trink—

We fall into a thousand-year sleep—

Yea, a long deep sleep for me and Trink. But I'll remember you Anya, I'll dream of you—

And will you cry through your hands and reverse the river for me, the memory of me—

I will—

Okay, sounds like fun. Let's go.

We linger in the Attic after the others have gone. Our focus is now on DeLeon, who is alone, drinking Chamomile tea.

We are watching him watch the movie projected onto the wall.

It is the 1942 film, *The Glass Key*, starring Alan Ladd and Veronica Lake, based on Dashiel Hammett's novel of the same name. DeLeon's father briefly worked with Dashiel Hammett at the Pinkerton Detective Agency. When he was seventeen and had just read Hammett's novel, *Red Harvest*, Deleon asked his father what Hammett was like. His father responded —There's no way of knowing what anyone's *really* like. He was a man who kept to himself. That's what he was like.

DeLeon had already screened *This Gun for Hire* (1942) and *The Blue Dahlia* (1946), two other noir films which featured Lake and Ladd.

DeLeon is staring at Lake's phosphorescent countenance but is thinking about Trink, has been thinking about him for most of the night.

He has been judiciously weighing the situation, and at 3:22 am, he decides to call in Joe and Max.

The waves, strident and white-maned, rumble in and break, hissing foam.

It's like champagne fizz, Anya says.

It's like a sperm bath, Piers says.

Eeewwl, that's disgusting, Anya laughs and scrunches her nose.

No it isn't, Piers protests, it's nature. And nature is natural and not disgusting, right?

Natural *can* be disgusting, Anya counters, but cites no examples.

Piers and Anya are standing barefoot on the shore. The ground beneath their feet registers as moist batter. The air is cool and studded with a briny wind.

Trink and the others are on the beach, about thirty feet away, playing Duck Duck Goose. The Cure's *"Just Like Heaven"* gospels out of a boombox:

Daylight licked me into shape
I must have been asleep for days
And moving lips to breathe her name
I opened up my eyes
And found myself alone alone
Alone above a raging sea
That stole the only girl I loved
And drowned her deep inside of me

Piers and Anya hold hands and stare out, as if waiting for a movie to begin.

I'm going in, Piers says.

She hitches up her pants to just above her knees.

You want to come in? Just a little ways?

I don't know. It's pretty cold.

Piers bends down and scoops sea-lather onto her index, brushes it against Anya's cheek.

Sea sperm, she teases.

Eeeewwl, Anya plays at being disgusted.

You won't be cold. You're an ice fairy. From the Ukraine. Remember?

Anya remembers and takes Piers's hand and they move forward together.

It's cold, Anya hunches her shoulders.

Piers says nothing, squeezes Anya's hand.

She looks down as the sea recedes, glugging and burbling, forking to either side of her ankles.

It's playing backwards, Piers notes with joy.

What?

Look down. Keep looking. And wait. Wait . . . wait . . . now.

Anya watches the sea reverse course, an aria sung inward.

It plays backwards, Anya delights. Like your river.

Like my river, Piers softly agrees.

Piers and Anya continue holding hands and continue staring down, keeping vigil to a rhythm.

The sea is the sea,

but it is also a sound recording of the sea.

It is Memory, shroud and fathomless

and freighted with echoes.

Anya feels shivery, plucked,

bare to the touch of the sea,

and wonders about mermaids, were they real, were they singing songs right now

that she couldn't hear, and why couldn't she hear them, and
would she ever hear them

and what kind of songs did they sing

were they elegies eulogies dirges

were they meant for us, were they

what did Piers think about mermaids, did she think

were they endangered extinct not there at all

Anya wanted to die

a death-feeling wringing her gut

but then just like that she was okay again

like the sea, mercurial yet bound to meter,

playing backwards and forwards backwards and forwards
backwards and

Piers, remote and slow breathing, stares out, as if trying to
translate something in the distance,

as if trying to translate distance itself.

At this point, everything grows blurry, out of focus.

When Piers was six, she fell into a well. The well was
abandoned and no longer had any water in it. If there had been
water in it, Piers would have drowned. Sometimes she'd imagine
that she had drowned, and that the life she went on living was a
haunted, unnatural one, a grave secret between her and the well.

Piers fell into the well chasing a white fox. A number of people,
including her Uncle Clark, told her that it must have been a gray
fox, a breed which was native to the area, that looked white in the
sunlight. Piers didn't argue but knew, without a doubt, that it was
a white fox, not a gray fox that looked white in the sunlight. Same
as she knew that it had multiple tails.

Piers believed that if she captured one of the fox's tails, her life would change, it would become different. She wasn't sure how exactly, she just knew it would.

She spotted the fox, or rather its shadow, first, near the edge of the creek that cut through her backyard. The shadow was projected onto the ground from behind some brush, and then came the fox, a shock of white, its multiple tails flaring like plumes of cloud.

Piers crept low to the ground and tried sneaking up on the fox, but that didn't work. Soon she was chasing it across an open field.

The well, located in the field, was about a 1/3 mile away from the house where Piers lived with her Uncle Clark and Aunt Sylvia. Sylvia, who was working in the garden, had no idea that her niece had gone off in pursuit of a white fox.

It was weird, Piers said. I thought the fox had gone into the well and I looked down and next thing I know I'm scrunched in the narrow dark at the bottom of the well. It didn't even feel as if I had fallen into the well. It felt like I had been beamed there. Except I knew I had fallen because of the pain in my leg, this dull hot throbbing pain that ran from my ankle to my thigh.

It's hard to say. I might've been down there thirty minutes, might've been three hours.

Time, sovereign and elastic, accelerates and decelerates according to the nature of circumstances. The qualities of light and dark and emotional climate are key variables.

According to the newspaper report, it is believed that Pierangela Lund, age six, was trapped in the well for approximately one hour.

I screamed and screamed until nothing was left inside. I had screamed myself wordless and soundless. Then I just stared up at the mouth of the well. It seemed so far-away, this disc of light, this gold coin. I knew that if I could reach this gold coin, there would be other gold coins, and air. But it was an impossible coin, one that I could only see not touch.

Then came the impossible boy and his stones.

Belle Fourche Gazette, July 26th, 1979: The boy, Emmet Grayson, who lived nearby, was wandering in the open field, playing by himself. "I was throwing stones into the well," Emmet explained, "it's this game I sometimes play, where I shoot the stones from different angles and see how many I can score in the well. Then I heard something coming out of the well. I got closer and it was screaming. It was freaky, I almost ran away, thinking it might be a ghost or monster or something."

That first stone got me pretty good. I even have a little scar, right here (Piers indicates a small waxy cleft just outside her right eyebrow). I didn't know what had happened. When other stones started raining down, I realized someone must be throwing them. That's when I found new screams inside me, the biggest ones yet.

Emmet ran to tell his parents, who told the authorities, who had already been looking for the missing Piers. Piers was pulled out of the well with a rope. For a while, people in town referred to her as the Girl from the Well. As if she had been born there.

The well incident indirectly led to Piers's relationship with puppets. At home, while her fractured leg mended, she made her first puppets, Booboo and Jean—a yellow and red sock, respectively—and they undertook many adventures without ever leaving Piers's hands. It was then that Piers found she could go into trances and take leave through Booboo and Jean.

Years later, Piers would see a news story about a mother who drowned her mentally disabled infant in a well and this would trigger an obsession in her about children who drowned in wells. She hadn't (there was no water) yet many had (drowned), some being accidents, some being murders. Piers began combing newspaper archives and collecting names, locations, birth and death-dates, along with whatever else she could find out about these children. Her Sad Ophelias. That's what she called them.

Boy or girl, it didn't matter, they were all her Sad Ophelias. She thought about the screams, all the ghosts of screams, fastened to thin air in those wells.

She told herself that one day she would take a pilgrimage, on foot, across the states and visit as many wells as she could find and leave stones there. Stones to honor any children who might have lost their lives in those wells, and if none had, then the stones would serve as tactile blessings, protective talismans.

Piers was, for a while, obsessed with collecting the names of the dead and with the notion of the pilgrimage, but eventually the obsession lost traction. She stopped looking for stories and collecting names, stopped charting the pilgrimage she wouldn't take.

Xerox of a newspaper clipping pasted into Piers's Journal, undated

Chicago Tribune, November 11th, 1900

Girl Drowns in a Well:
Lilly Bernt Falls into Water and Her Pet Dog Gives the Alarm to the Mother

After a search of nearly twenty-four hours the body of Lilly Bernt, the 15-year-old daughter of a railroad switchman, was recovered from the tank well at the Lassig Branch of the American Bridge Company units yesterday afternoon.

The girl fell into the well at 4 o' clock on Thursday afternoon, and the only witness to the drowning was the little black terrier, Spot, that was the child's constant companion. Lilly left her home at 958 Claybourn avenue, and, with a basket on her arm, she went to gather up enough chips to cook supper for the family. She was gone only a half-hour when the dog returned, and by means of whines and yelps made the mother of the girl understand that the child had met with mishap. Alex Bent, brother of the girl, followed the faithful little animal, and was led to the well, from which a large oil tank had recently been removed.

In her search for chips Lilly had gone to the Chicago and Northwestern railroad tracks that run by the bridge works yard. A large open gate at the Diversey avenue end of the

yards revealed what the girl thought to be a
pile of chips and wood that had been thrown
into the yard. She made her way in and,
setting the basket down, began to fill it
with scraps of wood.

The coveted chips, however, were but a
death trap. They were floating upon the
surface of eighteen feet of rain water and
had been deposited there to help fill up the
hole made by the reoval of the oil tank.

She evidently stepped on a block of wood
floating in the water and sank to the bottom.
A fire engine was used to pump the water so
that the baby could be recovered. Had it not
been for the sagacity of the dog, the child's
fate might never have been known.

(Piers's comments written below the clipping):

Is that the <u>real</u> story of Lilly Bernt? Is that how it happened?
How do they really know?

Stories are made or constructed to fill in the blanks. The wise
dog is the key to this story. Without the dog, there is only mystery.
Maybe one of those forever and ever mysteries. But because of the
dog there is a story with a beginning, middle, and end.

I wonder what the ghost of Lilly Bernt would have to say about
all this. I wonder what the ghost of Lilly Bernt *does* say about all
this. And no one's hearing her. Case closed.

Piers's Journal, February 2nd, 1983

Nine Tails of the Fox
by Pierangela

Kit was a very wise and ancient fox and had nine tails. To even have four or five was a big deal, but nine was tops.

No fox had more than nine. Nine was the cut-off. Each tail served a different purpose.

One tail was the charmer. It charmed with magic and creatures slipped right into its fox-hold.

Another tail was a flamethrower. If Kit was angry or under attack tail number two would spit flames as if from the mouth of a fierce dragon.

There was a tail that told tales. It was the storyteller. It knew all sorts of stories from all different times.

One tail made Kit invisible. Invisibility was very important for a fox.

Another tail could tell the fox what was coming. It was the seer.

Tail number six was a singer. It had a built-in jukebox.

The seventh tail was a tail of good fortune. Foxes thrive on good luck.

The eighth tail was a whisperer. It whispered messages to the wind and to other animals. The whispering made everything calm.

The ninth tail had no known use. It was the Tail of Eternity. It stood for everything and nothing.

Question to Piers: If you could have one of the fox tails, which one would it be? And why?

Answer: I would choose the whispering tail because the power to make everything calm would be a great power. Like how a mother sings a lullaby to put her baby to sleep. It would be a power like that.

P.S. Invisibility would be really cool too.

It was nearly dawn when Joe and Max arrived.

Modeling dark trench coats and fedoras, they looked very much the part they played, the parts they were about to play in handling the Trink Matter.

They were, same as the Winter's Brides, calculations arranged and composed according to DeLeon's vision and standards.

In wingtips, they ambled clumsily down a sand dune.

Over there, Joe pointed.

Trink and the Brides were lounging around a low-burning campfire.

Trink was melted, supine, his head cradled in the cushy lap of Bride Lulu, his temp-Mom.

Heavy with sleep, Trink lucidly slow-dreamed what had been a glorious memory from earlier in the night, when he had met one of his idols, Boy George, who had been in the audience at Tabanid. Trink had gotten his autograph and had taken a picture with him.

The Polaroid, like a heart-magnet, now rested squarely on Trink's chest:

Boy George, hair
a pinned-up rainbow
or My Little Pony manespray
tongue stuck-out aaaaaaahhh as
if modeling KISS
middlefinger arched & spearing
other arm slung round Trink's
shoulder
Trink beaming/smiling like he's
swallowed a star

Piers and Anya were perched on a lifeguard chair.

They had spent their time kissing, telling stories, devising metaphysical rescue plans for the Sad Ophelias, (Operation Ophelia Resurrect, was how Anya phrased it) kissing, swapping questions—what is it like to be an albino model? would you marry a mermaid if? did you always know you liked girls? why invisibility?

and kissing.

Their hands remained interlocked the entire time.

They were afraid to let go because, and when the pinkish milky light of dawn appeared, they became even more afraid, and held hands tighter, but when Piers saw the trench coats closing in on Trink & Co., she became afraid in a different way and let go of Anya's hand—

Piers, Anya cried out, opening and closing and opening and closing her fingers as if trying to recover something. Piers where are you—

But then she saw.

Two men, violently oppositional in tone and character, to the white-burning-white of the Brides, the whole thing a symbolic clash.

It went down like this and fast.

Joe ordered Trink to get up, and Trink bleated What the fuck, and Max said He said to get up, and then Max, the portlier of the two men, jammed his thumbs into Trink's armpits and forced him to rise.

By then Piers had come between the two men and Trink and said, fire in her voice, tiger in her eyes—You need to leave him alone.

Joe, at a lean six feet even, towered over Piers and turned to Max and smirked.

Max, adopting Joe's smirk, turned to Piers—You need to step

aside. This is going to happen.

Joe, angling his smirk—He's coming with us and that's that.

I don't wanna go with you, why do I gotta go with you, I don't wanna, Trink pleaded.

Joe calmly explained—If you go with us, you'll live, if you stay…

Joe let Trink finish the threat in his head.

Trink began torqueing and bopping in a self-contained space, running away without leaving.

Oh, come on man, why do I gotta go, I don't wanna go, come on man, you can't do this bullshit, come on.

The Brides, including Anya, remained quiet, terrified, and quiet, until Trink's temp-Mom, Lulu, spoke on his behalf—Can't you just leave him be, he's a gentle good soul?

Joe stared down at his shoes and shook his head while noting the pearls of sand that had collected on the tips of his shoes.

Max stared at Bride Lulu, then at the other Brides, and felt as if he had crashed a storybook, a fairytale. He blankly reiterated—He needs to go with us.

You fucking Nazis, Piers exploded and bent down, filling both her hands with sand, ready to hurl it into Joe's and Max's faces.

Joe's hand slid inside his trench coat, hinting at the gun he was carrying. Max mimicked Joe's action, on a two-second delay.

Joe: I'd seriously reconsider my decision, if I were you.

Max: It would behoove you to reconsider.

Piers remained indecisively frozen, and so badly didn't want Max and Joe to see that her hands were trembling, and her legs too, but she knew that they could see that their eyes owned her.

Oh, holy fuck, let's just go, Trink held out his hands, as if expecting Joe or Max to handcuff him.

First, I wanna see what the kid does with the sand, Joe cracked.

Yea, I wanna see how this plays out, Max said.

Let it go, babygirl, Trink cautioned.

Fucking hell, Piers growled and threw down the fistfuls of sand.

Babygirl I'm gonna be fine, just fine, Trink hand-on-the-shoulder consoled her. I got into a little bit of a mix-up, that's all, but it will get straightened out and, everything's gonna be fine-fine-fine. I'll pay the piper, and then 1990, babygirl, it's 19 fucking 90.

Joe and Max allowed the scene to run its course and then nudged Trink along.

The parting shot, sad and ludicrous, was that of two dark boxy trench coats sandwiching a thin, fairy-glittery black man, heading towards a sand dune, and then over onto a promenade, and then gone.

What do we do, Anya asked, call the police?

No, Piers snapped, no police.

What-do-we-do became the unspoken chorus, the feel, the death ray.

Everyone had been abruptly beamed from playtime into the middle of an unexpected funeral.

Some of the Brides turned to Piers, perhaps awaiting a cue, perhaps to sympathize.

Piers, after doing and saying nothing, picked up the boombox and walked away.

When there was enough distance between her and the Brides, she hit PLAY on the boombox,

listened to what Robert Smith was singing, hit STOP, flipped the tape, and forwarded it until she came to the song she needed to hear.

"Show me how you do that trick
The one that makes me scream" she said
"The one that makes me laugh" she said
And threw her arms around my neck
"Show me how you do it
And I promise you I promise that
I'll run away with you
I'll run away with you."

The tears, in reverse, ran.
Piers closed her hands and held them in.

DeLeon:

There are rules, codes. If those rules are broken, if those codes are violated, then there are consequences. Cause and effect. It's simple, really. People tend to make things way more complicated than they actually are. If you operate according to certain principles and allow those principles and not your moods or whims to guide your decisions, you can minimize needless complications.

In this particular situation: Trink owed me money. He owed me money and was given a due date and didn't pay. He was then extended a grace period, and he still didn't pay. He kept coming around to the club, feeding me excuses and alibis, and then even those stopped. He said nothing at all, like he was hoping the debt would magically vanish if we didn't talk about it. Things do vanish, but not magically.

My choice was to take punitive action, as any collection agency would, and let him know that I was not going away until his obligation was met. I would threaten, I would aggressively influence... yes, I admit that these are some of the ways in which I handle my affairs. It is the nature of the business I am in and I acknowledge and own that.

It took Joe and Max some time before they found the right alley. It had to be par for the course, and secluded, especially since they no longer had the cover of dark alley as an advantage.

They knew that DeLeon would have preferred this to have happened at night and not in the morning, but his specific instructions had been:

I want you to bring him into a dark alley, and no matter what goes down, Do Not, I repeat, Do Not allow this to occur to anywhere except in a dark alley. Understand?

They understood.

DeLeon, in prepping Joe and Max, specifically emphasized what he considered two masterful and menacing "alley" scenes, one from *The Set-Up* (1949) and the other from *On the Waterfront* (1954).

Joe and Max, whose real names were _________ and _________, had worked for DeLeon for the past five years. They were well-developed musical extensions of his *program*. DeLeon paid for their private acting classes, their dialogue coaching; he furnished them with syllabuses comprising *noir* and gangster films; he had spent a lot of time, energy, and effort in molding their characters and making certain that they functioned according to stylized design. The dark alley was yet another calculated convention in paying homage to noir.

Do you think it's dark enough, Joe asked Max, after having pulled into a narrow Chinatown alley.

It will have to be, Max said, we've been scouting locations for almost an hour and it's not getting any darker out.

It was when the car stopped that reality set in for Trink. He clutched the door-handle and began crying.

Joe: Save the waterworks till after we're through with ya.

Max: You deadbeats are all the same. You walk the walk, all

prissy and arrogant, I don't give a shit, this-that-and-this, then when it's time to pay the piper, you wanna tap out.

Max, in a moment of self-doubt, wondered if he had delivered his lines with enough conviction.

Joe, in a supple moment of self-reflection, recalled an incident in which he had gotten into trouble with his father and how he so badly wanted to escape the consequences (but couldn't) and briefly sympathized with Trink's desire for absolution, yet Joe didn't break character—Get out of the car, Cryboy.

Trink stayed where he was. Clutched the door handle even tighter. Tried to brave back his tears. He didn't want to die crying. He didn't want to die at all. He explained to Joe and Max—I don't want to die.

Joe deadpanned—You worry about the future too much.

Max admired Joe's line and his delivery of it.

Good one, Joe, Max said.

Thanks, Max, Joe smiled.

Max brandished his gun as incentive.

Trink got out of the car and stood up.

The alley was narrow and not exactly dark, but dark enough in that it was shadow-sandwiched between two tall buildings zigzagged with fire escapes.

Trink saw the quartered sheaf of light over Joe's and Max's shoulders, the temptation of exit. He thought about making a run for it. His legs wouldn't move.

Listen, I'll pay it back, Trink started, but the *—ck* of *back* flew out of his mouth like baby teeth when Max whaled a meaty fist into his gut.

Trink crumpled and hit the floor.

Joe and Max savaged him, mostly with their wingtips.

Piers's Journal, February 7th, 1990

Dear Trink,

This is the letter I would have sent you. If I knew where to send it.

It's been over a month. I don't know where you are, where you went.

I know that you are not dead. At first I thought maybe they killed you, but I can feel that you're still alive. Somewhere.

We had that special kind of bond between us from the beginning, didn't we? I could feel you and you could feel me, even from great distances. I can feel you now. I know that you are scared and lonely, and that breaks my heart, but I am glad you are still alive.

I've had nightmares, some awake, some asleep, about what the bastards did to you. In one of the nightmares they slashed your face with a razor, and I hope to god this isn't what actually happened, you have such a beautiful face.

I'm sorry I wasn't brave enough when they took you away. I wanted to be brave for you, but I wasn't. Not enough. I didn't stop them. It kills me inside. I think about it a lot. How if only I could have stopped them, if only.

The love between us was very pure, wouldn't you say? (So stupid, asking you a question knowing you're not gonna read this and that you can't respond… so be it, I'm stupid.)

Last week I got angel-wings tattooed on my back. Serrated, all dark.

Part of me did it to honor you and part of me did it to honor me. Until the real wings grow in.

You know I know I am a beautiful boy with wings, even if the surface is lying.

I remember saying that when I was really little. I am a beautiful boy with wings. I said it with my eyes closed, I remember that, too. Even then I knew that the mirror behind my eyes was much truer than the other mirrors.

I also remembered what you once said to me, you said there was a place between dreaming and awake and that's where I was, that's where you'd always find me and that's where you'd always love me.

Find me.

Or maybe that's where I need to go to find you. I don't know.

You know what, something came to me about a week ago and it's been building inside me and now I know I'm gonna do it. I'm going to make DeLeon pay. I'll tell you more about it after it's done.

I love you and miss you.

Your Wreck-mate, Piers

I rise
I always rise after the crucifixion
Bread and the wafer
Perfume and sperm I have lost my brother
Dark dark asleep asleep asleep
Floating floating again
Crucifixion
I kissed his shadow

—Text by Anaïs Nin, from *The House of Incest* (1936), used for the soprano voices in Edgard Varese's "Nocturnal"

Piers continued hanging out at Tabanid. She continued huffing Sike in the Attic.

The coat-nook remained an isolated enclave of pleasure.

There was Soozie, and there was Elyse. There was Lucy.

One night there was her mother, who she found and then lost again, just like that, a rabid blink and resurrection masquerading as a girl named Jean. There was Jean, and then Jean again.

Piers kept at it with clockwork regularity. On the surface everything seemed to be as it had always been, yet here was the difference: Piers watched. She kept strict vigil, and with intent.

She calculated, plotted, and rehearsed. And then one Tuesday night, she made her move.

The black-and-white footage of the hooded girl breaking into his office and robbing a briefcase felt unreal to DeLeon. He watched the footage over and over, waiting for reality to snap in. Eventually it did.

Piers had robbed him. Even with the hood on, he knew it was her and he was pretty sure she wanted him to know.

He wondered about the psychology behind her actions—Was it all about stealing Sike? Did part of it have to do with the violence perpetrated on Trink?

Ballsy. He had to give her that. This little thing picking the lock to his office, snatching the briefcase, scissor-snipping the cord to the telephone on his desk. And, just to needle him, an absentee fuck-you.

She had made her move and now it was on him.

DeLeon considered the different angles as he finished stirring the sauce.

Zoe, dinner, he called out.

In a second, dad, Zoe called back.

Zoe, DeLeon's nine-year-old daughter, spent most weekends with him. When she stayed over they had rituals. One of them was spaghetti and meatballs for dinner, followed by her favorite dessert: fudge brownies. The other ritual was watching a movie.

Zoe lined up the last of her Smurfs and then stood over them. Once she was satisfied that everyone was in the right place and that no one would move, she joined her father in the kitchen.

DeLeon set down two bowls of spaghetti on the table. Then he set down the salt and pepper shakers and a container of parmesan cheese.

Zoe snowed cheese all over her sauce. DeLeon seasoned his sauce with salt and pepper and applied a minimal amount of parmesan.

Zoe blew on the steam rising from her sauce, diverting its trajectory.

What are we watching tonight?

Labyrinth, Zoe responded between sauce-cooling exhales.

Again?

Dad, you watch movies like a thousand times.

That's an exaggeration.

Okay. Like 800 times.

That's better, DeLeon smiled.

Zoe twirl-wound a wad of spaghetti onto her fork, placed it in her mouth, swallowed.

Why, you wanna watch something else?

No, I'm just teasing, Labyrinth is fine. How many times have you seen it?

I don't know, maybe like twelve times.

DeLeon nodded, sipped his water. He looked at his daughter and thought of Piers. How she had robbed him. He tried to imagine his daughter as a thief and as a drug-addict. And what if she were both? What would he do?

What is it about Labyrinth, he asked Zoe.

What is it? Oh, you mean why do I keep watching it over and over?

Yea.

The Goblin King. He's so creepy-cool. Don't you think so?

Sure. You know he came into my club once?

Who, the Goblin King?

David Bowie, yes. He came in with this tall beautiful black woman. They both seemed like they weren't human.

Wow. What was he like? Did you talk to him?

A little bit. Hard to say what he was like. He didn't seem human. Maybe an alien. Or a vampire.

Or a goblin.

Or a goblin, yes.

Wow, that's cool, Zoe reached for the parmesan. You should have gotten his autograph.

Yea, I probably should have.

DeLeon watched his daughter unleash another blizzard of parmesan onto her sauce.

He felt confident that she would never become a thief or drug-addict.

Head Shot (Clip #6), March 16th, 1988

Face-shadow
  cast like
    ashprint upon
      faded white canvas

Black & white
close-up
back of shaved head
a fixed constellation
basking in celluloid for 2:37

Snapcrackly
crunch of the camera
running

This was the first time DeLeon had filmed Piers.

He had asked her if he could film her for his *Head Shot* series, which amounted to screen tests for his personal film collection.

Piers asked What would I have to do, and DeLeon responded Nothing. Just let me film your face for a couple of minutes.

Piers mused hmmm and maybe and then said she feared the camera was a mercenary and a thief and might steal something essential through her eyes, so would he consider filming the back of her head instead of her face?

DeLeon was amused and intrigued by Piers's logic and so he indulged her request.

He was surprised when, after watching *Head Shot* (Clip #6), how it moved and appealed to him so much more than the other

Clips, which was why he started filming people from behind, with the backs of their heads as the primary point of focus.

June, 1986

MISSING

Have You Seen This Girl?

Name: Pierangela Lund
Alias: Piers
Sex: Female
Age: 14
Height: 5'2
Weight: 105 lbs.
Hair: Chestnut brown
Eyes: Teal-gray

Piers was last seen on Thursday, June 19th, 1987, wearing a white Adidas sweat-jacket, beige carpenter pants, and purple Doc Marten boots.

If you have any information regarding Piers's whereabouts, please contact the Belle Fourche Police Department at: (605) 892-4353

Piers:

I am a runaway again. Or maybe it's—once a runaway, always a runaway?

Anyways at least I have wings this time.

I know DeLeon will come after me, knew that when I made the decision I made. It's part of the game. Cat and mouse. That's the way the game works.

I wonder where I'll go?

Too much wondering never got anyone anywhere. That's definitely something my Uncle Clark would say.

Well, wondering got Alice to Wonderland, didn't it, probably would have been my smartass reply. Anyways, I'm pretty sure Greyhound doesn't stop in Wonderland, so I'm gonna have to choose another destination.

Funny how I spent almost three years in L.A. and it only feels like a couple of weeks. I love it here and I'm gonna miss it.

If this were a fairytale, then L.A. would be the Kingdom, and DeLeon the evil monarch, and me… the what? Not the fucking princess, that's for sure. I'd be the urchin, no, I'd be the dark angel, no, I'd be the entertainment, the court puppeteer. Yea, that'd be me. The court puppeteer turned criminal, wanted dead or alive. Something like that.

I tell you though, I feel good about having wings on my back, they feel like a good omen. If you're gonna run away, it's better to have wings than to not have wings, right?

Piers's Journal, May 28th, 1987

It is my third day in L.A. I still can't believe I'm here. I've been sleeping in an abandoned house with a bunch of other people. All thanks to Rose.

I met Rose on the Venice Beach boardwalk, where she was playing songs on her guitar. It was my first day in L.A. and the thing I most wanted to do was to see the ocean. Someone told me which bus to catch to go to Venice Beach and he told me that there would be plenty of ocean for me to see. I loved that he had said plenty of ocean. It made me think of something that would never run out, something that wouldn't disappoint. Plenty of ocean.

Getting off the bus and walking and seeing palm trees everywhere… they looked fake to me, like props for a movie set. I was tempted to climb one and see what it was like up inside a palm tree, but I didn't want to get into trouble, not on my first day.

When I got to the beach, there she was: the mighty Pacific. And there was plenty of her. She was noisy and seemed to go on forever and wasn't blue, like I thought she'd be, but gray and green. The most beautiful gray-green I had ever seen. The gray-green of freedom.

I took off my boots and socks and walked in the sand and loved the transition between warm sand and cool shore. I rolled up my jeans and went in. The cold water felt good on my skin. I saw people swimming and two boys younger than me whacking a colored beach ball back and forth and it would bob like a buoy whenever it landed in the ocean. My ocean. Their ocean. All of ours. There was plenty for everyone. If the ocean was big, the world was even bigger, and I was now a part of it; free. I could go where I wanted, do what I wanted to do. All the shadows that had closed in on me in Belle Fourche were gone. I was in the sunlight, in the ocean, in L.A., by myself, and I was 14. Fucking nuts.

So, yea, Rose. After hanging out on the beach for a while I went to the boardwalk, which was crowded with all sorts of people. Like a big fucking party. I saw a woman with blonde dreads and a kerchief singing songs and playing guitar. I liked her raspy voice, so I sat and listened for a while. When she took a break, she came over and talked to me, said something about me reminded her of someone she once knew. She knew right away, without me saying, that I was a runaway. Said she was too, or she had been when she was younger (she asked me to guess her age, I guessed 33 and then 35. Was wrong twice, she was 37) and when she found out I had nowhere to stay, she invited me to stay with her. At first I thought that meant I'd be crashing at her place, but then found out it meant sleeping in an abandoned house with a bunch of other squatters. Rose said she had been staying in this house, which the residents called Mercy Central, for a while now. She played another set and then we walked to the store and Rose bought a case of beer and then we went to the beach where two of Rose's friends, Harmon and Pete, joined us. We drank beer and the two men and Rose took turns playing songs on her guitar. I got pretty drunk and walked up to the dark ocean, (it was night) and became obsessed with watching the white manes appear when the waves broke. Later I told Rose and Harmon and Pete it was like watching Neptune's horses storm in and the men laughed, but in a good way, and Rose said she liked the way I saw things. When we finished the beer, we left for Mercy Central.

Piers hadn't decided where she was going.

She looked at the list of different destinations on the terminal board, and looked and looked and picked Albuquerque because

she remembered as a kid watching a Bugs Bunny cartoon in which Albuquerque was mentioned except Bugs called it 'Albakoikey' so she bought a ticket to Albuquerque.

As the bus slow-rolled out of the dark and into daylight, Piers felt many things at once.

She felt relieved. She felt scared. She felt worried. She felt impossible.

She side-glanced a fat woman in the seat across from her staring.

She met the gaze of the fat woman, whose eyes skittered away.

Piers stood up and took the briefcase down from the overhead compartment and put it under her seat, allowing the heels of her Docs to make contact with its edge. Then she unzipped her backpack, took out a small umber vial and cloth, and went to the bathroom.

Several minutes later she returned to her seat. She looked over at the fat woman, who was reading a paperback. She tried to make out the title of the book but couldn't. Probably a trashy romance novel, she guessed.

She stared out the window and saw palm trees and people and cars and buildings. The afternoon haze was specter-tint.

The bus motored along, and she continued staring out, remembering that someone had once said you see more of life if you're looking through one window than if you're looking out many windows.

There it is, the fullness of L.A., appraised through a single window, a personal peephole.

As the light sheathing the window changed and Piers saw her

image reflected back to her, a watery phantasmal reflection, she felt as if she were a ghost, simply passing through.

The palm trees and the people and the cars and the buildings, those things were real, but she was not.

This notion set Piers at ease, made her feel unshackled, as if she could anywhere she wanted anytime and nothing could ever happen to her, not really.

I kept skating in and out of consciousness, not really falling asleep but more like this half-sleep or fugue or something, and every time I'd see these nefarious men, well not actually see 'em, but more like I had a sense of 'em, and these men drugged me and abducted me and were transporting me across the country to other nefarious men who wanted me. Why did they want me? What had I done? It was so hard to wrench myself out of these stupors, but I did, and whenever I did and saw that I was on the bus, I felt so happy, I told myself Stay Awake, but I'd fall back into the nefarious men, the terror.

Then there was the night scream, which hadn't come from me. I was stranded in one of my bad dozes and all-of-a-sudden there's this scream that cut right into me and my heart jumped into my throat. It was the fat woman. She screamed like she was dying, followed by several low moans and that was that, show over. I looked at the fat woman. She wasn't moving. Was she dead? No, her chest was heaving. What had she dreamed? Something about nefarious men? Or..?

Piers was glad the seat next to her was empty.

She braced herself against the window side and stretched out longways and put on her headphones.

Arabic-laced guitar-riff

prompting David Bowie's

genie-in-a-vacuum
voice singing a song about
The Man Who Sold the World.

. . . .

Although I wasn't there
He said I was his friend
Which came as a surprise
I spoke into his eyes
I thought you died alone
A long long time ago

It was vague and abstract and yet the felt-sense was resonant:

a herd of giant red lions, female cuz none of 'em had manes,
running through the sky.

It was like the lions were made from clouds or sand or some
other primordial element.

It had been the deepest sleep Piers had fallen into while riding
on the bus, sleep that felt like actual sleep and not a bad doze
omened by nefarious men. And so that morning when the bus
driver announced Redline as one of the stops, which Piers
misheard as Red Lion, she decided to get off there instead of
Albuquerque.

Piers's Journal, February 15th, 1990

And the stars faded,
and the child went away

Where I am going,
you cannot follow

Piers Wuz Here

A Brief Overview of Redline

The population of Redline is 5,201

Coal-mining, paper-making, and the manufacturing of telephone equipment are three staple forms of industry in Redline.

A number of mines have closed down, but many remain active. Generations of men have been employed as coal-miners in Redline, and this occupation continues even with a sooty skeletal hand knocking on the door of the 21st century.

Redline's name derives from its reddish complexion. That is: when the winds blow strong and fierce, as they do in the springtime, the red sands of the desert are whipped up into dust-clouds of red. A candychalk red, the red of spider's bites and religious sermons. And the horizon line, as seen through a dust-screened frame of vision, is also red. Redline.

There is a nuclear lab and research facility about forty miles west of Redline. The inside gallows' joke is that the town's natural red has undergone a toxic make-over. It is now a radioactive Kool-Aid red, the red of carcinogenic apples.

Redline's population is predominantly white and Hispanic. The Spanish settlers arrived in the late 1700s and placed their stamp on the town's ranching and agricultural identity.

There are several pueblos outside of Redline. The pueblo natives don't have much to do with the town unless they need to go shopping or drink at one of the bars. "Redline" has another name, its original indigenous one, but it is a secret name and it is no longer spoken.

The town is hemmed in by mountains, forests, valleys, and desert. The mountains are known as the Blue-Caps because of the indigo and midnight blue color that bruises its peaks during certain times of day, in certain slants of light. And one specific mountain, the goliath fronting the north side of town, is known as Blue-Mother, or Madre Azul.

There are outlying badlands. The badlands are sometimes referred to as the Crane Badlands, because petroglyphs of cranes were found in some of its caves.

There are people who believe that the Crane Badlands were the original location of Eden. A group known as Edenites, founded and led by a gentleman named Joseph Krantz, pay homage to the badlands of lost Eden through song and dance, prayer and rock-sculpture.

The only tourist draw to Redline is its surrounding nature, its badlands.

Cougars, the town's unofficial totem-animal, are solitary, secretive, and crepuscular. They can jump up to twenty feet into the air and run thirty-five to forty-miles per hour. Cougars cannot roar. They purr, like housecats, and are also known to scream, squeak, hiss, and whistle. There are over forty different names for the cougar, including: mountain lion, puma, deer tiger, fire cat, catamount, painter, and mountain screamer. No animal has more names.

There is a small, faded plaza in the center of town. What was once a thriving town square is now the thumbprint of a ghost. The town council has been discussing plans for its revitalization. Stay tuned.

One of Redline's earliest mayors, Clem Willoughby, wrote a book about the outlaw, Thomas "Black Jack" Ketchum. As the legend goes: Ketchum once passed through Redline and got involved in a high-stakes poker game at Trilby's Saloon (now a Burger King) and lost a lot of money. After the game broke up, Ketchum tailed the big winner, Earl Dodson, back to his room at Land's Inn (which is still Land's Inn) and shot Dodson in the back, killing him. Ketchum took back only the amount of money he had lost and left the rest for scavengers.

Ketchum was hanged on April 26th, 1901, in Clayton, New

Mexico. He was the first and only person ever to be hanged in New Mexico for the crime of train robbery. His hanging was a botched affair, the rope was too long, and Ketchum had packed on the pounds during his stint in jail. He was decapitated. His last words, as reported by the San Francisco Chronicle, were: "Good-bye. Please dig my grave deep. All right, hurry up."

Some archived photos representative of Redline:

Brush,
like parched pompadours
frizzing an otherwise bald
Martian-red sandscape.

Vogel's Gas Station, est. 1919.
The inflatable pink flamingo
you see is the station's mascot, Plink.
Charlie Vogel, Jr.,
third-generation owner of Vogel's
introduced Plink in 1985
saying *I figgered*
a flamingo would lighten things up
ya know
bring a touch of the exotic the tropical
to our little town
not to mention Plink
makes people smile so…

Clem Willoughby, jowly
& whiskered, holding up
the famed black & white photo
of Black Jack Ketchum
decapitated.

Twin smokestacks
coughing up plumes
of pipesmoke
arcing diagonally
toward a woolen skiff
of clouds
(Earth meeting Heaven
in an abracadra puff,
or do angels
get lung cancer, asked six yr old
Sally Gomez once,
Sally reputedly touched in the head)

The Shadow
of a formidable wingspan
inking a stubbled block
of desert.
The wings belong to a Pterodactyl,
gliding by overhead.
No one knows the date
this photo was taken,
nor the identity of the photographer
behind the myth.

Winter,
a tawny reddish-brown cougar,
idling horizontally on curds of snow.
Notice the primacy of its gaze,
ancient and razored, slowchewing Time.
Notice the light snow falling,
like bleached curlicues,
like frosted lashes.

A broken-down
brick-red Ford truck,
sunlight kissing
its scabrous rust.

It is hard to see
the man and woman
overexposed
in the milkbath of light,
but allegedly
this photo captures
Adam and Eve
right after Eden dissolved.

The interior of Red's diner.

Late morning.

Henry Hook, stoop-shouldered, seated at the counter, a plate of eggs over-easy, toast, and home fries, cup of coffee, newspaper spread out before him.

He is reading an article on the recent dissolution of the U.S.S.R.

The article made him think of the movie *Red Dawn*, about teenagers protecting their hometown from a Soviet invasion.

More coffee, Henry, Gwen held a coffee-pot at half-tilt over his cup.

Sure, Gwen, thanks.

Gwen poured.

What's new in the world, she asked.

Same ol', same ol', Henry looked up from the newspaper.

Sounds about right, Gwen smiled.

How's Jason doing?

Jason was Gwen's twenty-year-old son.

He's good. Finished the academy about six months ago and now they've got him stationed in Biloxi.

Send him my regards.

I will.

Gwen wheeled to go, and Henry asked—Hey Gwen, remember that movie Red Dawn?

Yea, that was the one about the kids fighting off the Russians, right?

Yea. Do you remember the name of main kid in the movie? I mean the name of the actor?

Gwen pursed her lips and knitted her brows.

No, I don't. But I'm terrible when it comes to remembering names of actors.

Yea me too, Henry chuckled. Thanks anyway.

Gwen went around refilling coffees.

The metallic singing of the bell from the front door opening drew Henry's attention to the mirror behind the counter. He saw her, the girl he had seen at Wal-Mart about a week ago. He had been stocking merchandise when he noticed a girl with a shaved head, a tiny thing swimming in a large gray overcoat, robbing items from the shelves.

Henry kept his eyes on the mirror as the girl approached the counter.

There was something about her eyes, something strange. There was too much of something in them.

She sat down on the stool, one over from his.

A tangy musk, like an animal that had been bathed in vinegar, came off the girl.

Henry shook a packet of sugar, tore it open, and poured the granules into his coffee. He repeated this, with a second packet of sugar, and then stirred.

He flipped through the newspaper and landed in the sports section. An article about Buster Douglas, the boxer who had recently dethroned "Iron" Mike Tyson.

Gwen appeared.

What can I get for you hon?

Piers's eyes darted this way and that, as if she were, crash-course-style, attempting to assimilate the various elements comprising the diner, its reality.

Coffee, she said.

Piers laid a gloved hand on the counter. The glove was fingerless, frizzy-wooly, and brown.

Her other hand, along with the rest of her left arm, was bound in a sling.

Gwen set down a cup of coffee.

Piers briefly made eye contact with Gwen and thanked her. Gwen smiled and shuffled away.

Piers removed five packets of sugar from the glass caddy and emptied them into her coffee.

Next, she poured in a generous amount of milk and used the handle-side of the spoon to stir.

Watching the whirlpool effect of black-to-cream-brown gave her a curious feeling, a sedate one.

She placed the handle-side of the spoon in her mouth and sucked off coffee-glisten.

She gulped her coffee, finishing most of it one sip.

She reached down for her backpack.

Unzipped it.

Took out a pen and a yellow notebook, and began writing.

Piers's Journal, February 27th, 1990

I am sitting in a diner that belongs to another era.

Even the music playing on the radio, big band swing, is from another era.

Have I traveled back in time?

Life is strange.

How A leads to B and then to C and suddenly you're at X and you're like how the fuck did I wind up here?

Here in this case being Red's diner in a town called Redline. Was the diner named Red's because the town was Redline? And why Redline? As for why I'm here, it's because while riding the bus I dreamed of red she-lions running across the sky. I repeat: Life is strange.

While I'm writing this, I need to thank goddesses that it was my left arm that went bad and not my right, otherwise I wouldn't have been able to journal. Or I guess I could have, but the writing would have just looked like the writing of an alien or a retard.

What happened to my arm? Nothing like this has ever happened before. It's like it's frozen or something. What the hell's going on?

The waitress just refilled my coffee. She has pretty eyes. They're pale green with bits of yellow in 'em. Or maybe they look pale-green with bits of yellow in this light. Her hair is faded platinum. I like her full bosom.

Are you my mother, I want to say to her, as a joke, as a play on that Dr. Seuss book, with the lost baby bird that goes around asking all the animals, Are you my mother? Are you my mother? Are you my mother?

The waitress smells of milk. Pink-smelling milk. Not regular milk but the milkman bringing fresh milk to your doorstep like in the old days. So maybe it's the memory of milk.

The man sitting next to me has an eye-patch. I wonder why?

What does he smell like? He smells like bacon. No, not bacon, salt. Like he's been rolling around in salt. Like salt, and like my uncle's woodshop.

While writing this I noticed an old man at a table staring at me in the mirror. I bet he thinks I'm a curious specimen. Where did she come from, this little bald-headed rat who's writing in a notebook? What is she writing? Is she writing about me?

Know what I did Trink? Looked into the mirror and stuck my tongue out at the old man. He shook his head and looked away. Pretty sure he thinks I'm a deranged vagrant. Maybe I am deranged vagrant.

Trink, I wish you were here so we could play deranged vagrants together.

Piers closed her journal and adjusted her bad arm, which was starting to ache.

Gwen refilled her coffee for a third time—Where you from honey?

Piers hesitated before responding—L.A.

Oh, okay. I spent some time in Los Angeles.

Piers nodded, unsure what to say.

Gwen went on—It was many, many years ago. I must've been around your, how old are you?

Twenty-one, Piers lied on beat.

Henry glanced the girl in the mirror. Twenty-one? No way. She couldn't have been more than. . . sixteen? seventeen?

Well, I was younger than you when I was there. I was sixteen.

Gwen was an actress on a TV show, Henry piped in.

Oh wow. What show?

It was called All Through the Years, Gwen said. Chances are you never heard of it. It was a program that ran in the 50s.

The syncopated chirping of a bell caught Gwen's attention.

Excuse me, gotta grab that order.

Gwen hustled away.

Henry went on, as if Gwen's proud personal historian—Yea, Gwendolyn Parker as Elizabeth Starling. That was the name of the family in the show, the Starlings. Gwen played the teenage daughter, Elizabeth, but only for one season. But that one season was enough to make her the #1 crush of teenage boys across America. There was even a fan club. We Love Gwendolyn Parker.

Piers shifted her attention to Gwen, holding two plates aloft as she delivered them to a table. She tried to imagine the middle-aged woman, whose attractiveness now bore a time-worn quality, as the beautiful teenager that had become a fan club icon.

Why only one season, Piers asked Henry.

Said she didn't want to do it anymore. She thought she wanted to be an actress and then she realized she didn't. Said she missed home. Ask Gwen about it, she'll tell you the story.

C. Thomas Howell, Gwen said as she cruised past Henry.

C. Thomas Howell? Who's that?

Gwen finished dropping off creamer at the table where she had delivered the plates, then explained to Henry—That's the name of the actor from Red Dawn. C. Thomas Howell. Bill just told me.

Henry acknowledged Bill, an old-timer in a cowboy hat, seated at a nearby table.

Good memory, Bill, Henry said to him.

This one's got a memory like an elephant, said his wife, Charlotte, who was seated across from her husband, buttering his toast.

Bill smiled and said nothing.

While this exchange happened Piers had returned to her journal, and in the right-hand margin of the page she had written on earlier, she wrote

Gwendolyn Parker
pretty eyes
and pink-milk-smelling
former actress
on 1950s TV show
All Through the Years
wet dream
of American teenage boys

You a writer, Henry asked.
No, but I've been journaling since I was little.

Henry sipped his coffee, then asked—Are you, is this your first time in Redline?

Um-humh.

You visiting someone?

No. How'd you get your eye-patch?

How'd I get it?

Why do you wear one?

Lost the eye—

Let me guess, in a bar fight?

Henry chuckled—No and yes. It was a bar fight, but I wasn't the one fighting. I happened to get in the way of a broken bottle meant for someone else's face.

Wrong face at the wrong time?

Piers smiled and Henry laughed.

That's a good one. You're quick.

Henry fixed his gaze on Piers's slingbound arm.

And your arm?

Piers looked down, as if needing to observe the sling to understand to what Henry was referring.

Some guys got rough with me, Piers practically whistled the words over Henry's shoulder. I'd rather not talk about it.

Henry nodded.

Piers asked Henry where the restroom was.

Over there, he pointed.

Piers took her backpack and went into the restroom.

She sat on the toilet.

Fumbling with one hand she unscrewed the cap from the vial, poured Sike onto her cloth, and huffed. And huffed some more.

She remained stock-still on the toilet.

She stared straight ahead.

She noticed that the name *Wanda* was carved onto the wooden door.

The letters began to move.

She closed her eyes.

This is your special raincoat, the woman said to her, the little girl, staring up at the woman who was hanging the yellow raincoat on a wooden peg to the right of the door.

So when it rains...

The woman's voice trailed off.

The woman toggled the girl's nose, then opened the door, walked out, and closed the door behind her.

The girl looked up at the yellow raincoat hanging on the wooden peg.

It looked bright, empty and sad.

The girl stared at the closed door, and beyond.

Are you my mother

Are you my mother

Are you my mother

Piers opened her eyes.

Wanda cut jaggedly into wood.

Piers put away her vial and cloth and left the restroom.

When she got back to the counter, the man with the eye-patch had gone.

Gwen came over, coffee-pot in hand.

More coffee?

Sure.

Gwen poured. Then turned to leave.

Excuse me what was the name of the man who was sitting next to me?

Henry. That was Henry.

Thanks.

Gwen smiled, left.

Piers opened her journal and in the right-hand margin, below what she had written about Gwendolyn Parker, she scribbled

Henry

a man

with an eyepatch

seems nice enough

We Love Gwendolyn Parker Fan Club
October 12th, 1956
3437 Orchard Drive
Burbank, CA 91504

Dear Gwendolyn,

I know you receive a lot of letters. I know mine will just be one in the hundreds or thousands that you get. Still I had to write it. I've never written a fan letter before. In fact this is the first letter I've ever written to anyone. I am a big fan of All Through the Years and am also a big fan of you. Every week I tune in and look forward to entering the home of the Starlings to see what's going to happen. The family gets into fixes, especially you and your brother Buddy. Well I guess I mean Elizabeth and her brother Buddy. Yet by the end of the show everything always gets worked out. And the family usually works it out together. That is very ~~reassuming~~ reassuring. One of the reasons I tune in is to get reassured. The other reason is you. Your portrayal of Elizabeth breaks my heart and lifts it up. I don't think I can explain why. Words are not my best way of expressing myself. Elizabeth is smart and clever and perky, she is all those things but there's something else to her. I guess the only thing I can call it is heart. You can feel Elizabeth's heart. It comes through. And in feeling Elizabeth's heart I can feel my own heart. I don't know if that makes any sense.

I won't ramble on. I just wanted you to know that I am a fan and I appreciate what you do. I am looking forward to season 2 of All Through the Years.

Fondly,
Henry

Pictures reflecting "yellow as an essential feel" pasted into Piers's Journal, Undated

Van Gogh, *Wheat Field with Crows*, 1890

What you might call
omen-brushed yellow, a virulent
scare, its quotient graded just
below dark, and subtly so.
A sky raining crows,
like a scandal of mustaches,
or handlebar dissent.
Yellow crosses
daring a blight,
or braving a mouthless ebb,
Agony and Ecstasy, yes

John William Godward, *Girl in a Yellow Drape*, 1901

In a state of honeyed repose,
her flightless body,
a constellation,
draped in the sheer cloth
of sunlight, as she models
hidden grief
to witnesses
unseen
by common sight

Mark Rothko, *Untitled* (Yellow and Blue), 1954

In this lighted instance,
a storm-watch of gold,
bearing the heft of silence
and time, slowed.
Blue
shoulders the collapse
of heaven,
it is the Atlas underlay,
the muscle-cloud formation
and tindered vault.

Georgia O' Keefe, *Green, Yellow and Orange*, 1960

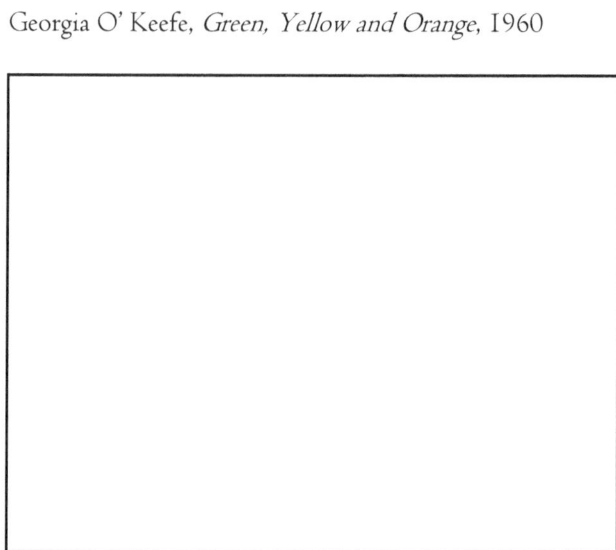

Upon a citrus-infused sky,
bright and sorry,
the dance of acidic vapors and
serpentine ravels, assuming
the burden of a faceless woman,
basking

Andy Warhol, *Banana*, 1966

A religious protuberance,
a monkey's Marxist gag.
To be eaten, to be peddled,
to be inserted or diagnosed,
a digestible comic device,
precursor to aerial pies
and throwaway wives.
As pop art,
it flirts and models
assumed vanity:
skin of siren-yellow,
a husky viscera,
negligeed in black tatters,
zealous tip hinting
at its decorous appeal,
implying an androgynous
grip on cinema
and Eden.

Henry:

I guess I took her in because, I don't know, I guess she kind of reminded me of my dog, Jacques. What I mean by that is, when I found Jacques, he was a stray, he had this look in his eyes that really-really called out for home. It was a true needing of home, ya know? So yea, something about her reminded me of Jacques.

Anyways I saw her again at Wal-Mart, stealing again, but she didn't see me, and after she left I thought about following her out but I wasn't sure what I would say to her, but then I figured she'd get scared so I didn't follow her. I talked to Gwen about her and Gwen said she had showed up at Red's a couple of days ago and she drank like six or seven cups of coffee and mostly wrote in her notebook and one time she asked Gwen, kinda out of the blue, why she quit acting, and Gwen told her the story and then she asked Gwen if she had a picture of herself when she was younger. Gwen said she didn't, and that was that.

About a week later, I saw her for the third time at Wal-Mart. I went up to her and said hello, she was surprised to see me. You work here, she said, and I nodded and asked her how she was getting along, she said, Fine, and then I asked her how she was finding Redline, she said, It's okay for now. Her eyes were everywhere, just dancing all over the place, and she kept rubbing her nose, and I wondered if she was sick or on drugs and when I asked her if she was okay she said, Yea, fine just been camping out and it gets cold as fuck out there at night, ya know, and I said, Yea I know, and the idea of this kid freezing her ass off camping at night made me wanna offer her my place as a place to crash, but I guess I didn't want to come off as some weird old pervert. Instead I said, How's your arm doing? She shrugged, It's okay, and I couldn't think of anything else to say so I asked her if she needed help finding anything in the store, and she said, Yea, where I can find razors, and I told her, Aisle 2, and she said, Just kidding I don't need any razors, then she asked me if I might be willing to put her up for a couple of nights, was that possible. . . I told her yea, no problem, and to come back to the store at five, that's when I got off from work, and we'd drive over to my place. It was a trailer that I shared with my dog Jacques.

Piers's Journal, March 15th, 1990

It is my fifth day crashing in Henry's trailer. It feels good to not be sleeping out in the cold and it's good for my arm too which remains frozen. It just locked into this position, like it's petrified or something, and I can't move it. I am definitely concerned, but I think it will get better soon. It has to.

I haven't played with any of the puppets I brought with me (though I did have a dream the other night in which the Golem appeared. I can't remember much except that he was this featureless orb weighing down on my chest, he was so-so heavy. At one point, he forced his way into my mouth and down my throat, I felt like I had swallowed a really cold knot, and that's all I remember). I need to make more puppets, but I haven't been motivated with my arm being fucked and all. Oh well.

I'm more concerned about how quickly my Sike supply has diminished. I figured a briefcase-full would last a while, but scratch that. It's gonna be done a lot sooner than I expected. I really-really need to try and slow down my rate of huffing. SLOW THE FUCK DOWN PIERS. There, let's see if that helps.

Henry's trailer is this rusty old orange and white metal worm from the 70s. It's located on the edge of town so if I want to go into town I need to catch a lift with Henry or hitch a ride, otherwise the walk is forever.

I've mostly just hung out in the trailer and taken short walks around the "neighborhood". All that's really out here is lots and lots of sagebrush and bushes and dirt and dust and trees. The landscape seems super thirsty. Like it's dying for a drink and is dehydrating into all sorts of muted browns.

Sometimes Jacques, Henry's dog, will walk with me, but not very far. Jacques is almost seventeen and, like Henry said, he's not much longer for this earth. You can tell that these two are best friends. I can also tell that Jacque's death is gonna leave a huge hole in Henry's heart.

When I first got here I wondered if Henry was gonna try something on me, if he was some sort of lonely old trailer-living dude who was hoping to cop young flesh.

I was worried but not really cuz something told me he was an okay guy, that he wasn't like that, and so far that's been true, and I hope that part of me is right and it continues to be true.

Henry's last name is Hook, which I think is cool and hilarious. And his father was in the navy, so in a way his dad was Captain Hook. When I told Henry this he laughed and said he'd never thought of it that way before. I think he likes having me around. But why? Maybe for the same reason he likes having Jacques around. Company. Duh.

I'm going a little crazy just hanging out in the trailer and taking walks in Nowheresville.

But at the same time, there's nothing else I wanna do, nothing else I can do, not sure why. I feel like I need to stay in or close to the trailer. If I don't, something bad will happen to me. Like what Piers? Like maybe a fucking Pterodactyl will swoop down from the sky and take me away. It sounds crazy, but this place has that kind of feeling. Like it's not entirely out of the realm of possibility for someone to be abducted by a Pterodactyl. Fucking weird.

I can hear the wind outside raging. Huge gusts are rattling the panels of the trailer. A few days ago, I saw why they call this town Redline when the winds kicked up clouds of red sand and dust that seemed to cover everything. Very demonic, very apocalyptic.

Think it's time to put down the pen and huff some Sike. And listen to The Cure. Yea it's definitely a Cure kind of day.

P.S. Holy shit, just realized today is March 15th. The Ides of March. Well that explains a lot.

Henry entered the trailer carrying a large brown bag.

He saw Piers sitting on the couch, her legs tucked beneath her, a yellow sock gloving her hand.

Startled by Henry's presence, Piers erupted into a half-laugh half-scream—You caught us.

Caught you?

Booboo and I were talking. This is Booboo.

Piers waggled the yellow sock.

Henry moved closer and saw that the sock had two black buttons sewn on for eyes and a flatline mouth drawn on in black marker.

Booboo, say hello to Henry, Piers said to Booboo, who said to Henry in a high-pitched and scratchy voice—Hello Henry.

Hello Booboo, Henry sheepishly acknowledged, feeling self-conscious about both talking to a sock and referring to that sock as Booboo.

I got Chinese, Henry said to Piers. You hungry?

Starved, Piers said.

She peeled Booboo from her hand and set her on the couch.

Henry crossed from the carpet into the linoleum-tiled kitchen and placed the bag on the table.

Jacques, who was lying near the couch had expectantly raised his head when Henry came in and awaited his cue.

Henry dropped to one knee—Come say hello, old boy.

Jacques elevated on creaky legs and made his way to Henry, who scratched behind his ears and massaged his scalp.

We took a pretty long walk today, Piers said. All the way to the cattle guard.

Wow, Henry glowed into Jacque's eyes. You got some life left in those old legs yet, huh?

Henry braced against the edge of the table and rose to

standing.

He removed two cartons, a plastic container, and two cans of Sprite from the bag.

I got pork lo mein, chicken fried rice, wonton soup, egg rolls, and Sprite. How's that sound?

Sounds great, thanks.

Piers joined Henry in the kitchen.

Henry started fixing their plates.

Can you get us two bowls for the soup?

Piers got two small bowls from the cabinet and placed them on the table.

Thanks, Henry said. Here—

He slid a paper plate loaded with noodles and rice toward Piers.

Thanks Henry.

Piers sat down.

You want chopsticks?

Sure.

Henry handed Piers chopsticks.

Watching her slide the chopsticks out of the red wrapper, he asked—How's your arm doing? Any better?

The same.

What did the doctors say? Is it fractured—

I didn't go to the doctor.

Henry nodded, tipped soup from the container into a bowl, a wonton kersploshing in the transfer. He slid the bowl toward Piers.

Do you want to see a doctor here?

No. I'm not into doctors.

Henry chuckled—Can't say I blame you. Here I am pushing

a doctor on you when I haven't been to one in, well, it's been a long while.

Henry sputtered a raspy cough, punctuated by wheeze— Look, I even mention a doctor and my chest starts acting up.

Henry laughed, igniting a series of motorboat coughs.

He went to the sink and spit. He looked down at the spit, as if analyzing it, then turned on the faucet and washed it down the drain.

Sorry about that, Henry said

Doesn't bother me, Piers shoveled a clump of noodles into her mouth.

Every time I get to coughing like that, makes me wanna immediately light up a cigarette. Weird, huh?

No, I don't think it's weird. It's called perverse pleasure.

Well I don't know about all that, but okay. Perverse pleasure.

Henry sat in his chair. He looked down at Jacques, who was staring longingly at the food.

Henry gave Jacque's scalp a rub—Don't worry, boy, you'll get taken care of.

As a show of good faith, Henry broke his egg roll in two— Start with that.

Jacques gentled the half-egg roll from Henry's palm and gobbled it in one bite.

Piers, who was now hunched over her plate, wolfed down her food without looking up, chewing minimally. When she was done, she downed most of her Sprite in a single sip and exploded a big burp.

She smiled—I eat and drink fast.

Like the world is coming to an end, Henry smiled back.

Henry ate, fumbling with his chopsticks, and Piers laughed— That's not how you hold chopsticks.

It's how *I* hold chopsticks, Henry smiled.

Let me show you.

Piers demonstrated with her chopsticks, which functioned like fluid pincers.

Henry tried to mimic the action but couldn't get it.

Maybe it's because you're left-handed, Piers suggested.

Yea maybe it's that, Henry agreed.

He set down the chopsticks and opted for a plastic fork.

You're giving up already?

You can teach me another time. I'm too hungry to learn right now.

Henry ate at his slow and deliberate pace.

Piers toggled the tab on her can of Sprite until it snapped off. She considered the tab then flipped it onto the table.

You know what was weird, Henry, when you came home earlier and I was talking with Booboo, I got freaked out in the way I used to get freaked out when I was little and my Uncle Clark would catch me talking to Booboo. Or Jean. Jean's my other sock puppet. He didn't like it.

Why not?

Because he thought something was wrong with me. In the beginning it was okay, but when I kept at it and he saw how much time I spent talking to them. . . he thought it wasn't normal for a girl to be talking to her socks all the time.

A laugh, not too far removed from a whimper, steamed through Piers's nostrils.

I think he thought I was possessed or something.

Possessed?

Yea, by like, demons. He used to call my puppets the devil's playthings. Can you imagine that? A grown man scared of a pair of colored socks?

Piers smiled, drained the remainder of her Sprite, continued—When he started threatening that someone would come and take me away, said there was a doctor who would come and take me to a special home, I started playing with Booboo and Jean in secret. But sometimes he'd catch me and then all hell would break loose. My Aunt Sylvia would try and calm him down, I'd hear her telling him it was just a phase I was going through, that I'd grow out of it. I knew he thought I was defective because I was my mother's daughter. You have any more Sprite?

No, that's it. You want some of mine?

Maybe just a little sip?

G'head.

Piers sipped and kept sipping and when she stopped—Sorry. Guess that was a big little sip.

That's okay. So, your mother?

My mother was a junkie. She couldn't raise me, so she gave me to her sister to raise me.

How old were you?

Three.

And your father?

Never knew him. Sperm donor.

Piers got up and walked over to the framed picture set on the counter, next to the microwave.

A black and white photo of a gangly, grinning young man, in a white sailor's outfit and cap.

Piers tapped the glass with her fingernail—There he is, Captain Hook. When was this taken?

I think around 1923. Before he set sail for the first time.

Piers lifted the picture, held at an angle, studied it. Then she put down the photo and rejoined Henry at the table.

It's a great photo. Did you want to be like your dad? I mean did you wanna join the navy?

Yea, I did. When I was a kid that's all I could think about. Growing up and joining the navy.

And what happened?

I grew up and didn't join the navy.

Because?

I don't know. I guess, I guess I lacked the necessary motivation or ambition or something. Whatever that something was, I didn't have it.

Piers nodded, picked up the empty Sprite can, squeezed it, put it down.

You've lived in Redline your whole life?

Yep. Well except for three months when I lived in Albuquerque. I wanted to try it out, but it wasn't for me. Too busy, too much of a city.

Wow. Wonder what you'd think of L.A?

I think it would be a nightmare. But you loved L.A., huh?

I loved it, yea.

Do you think you'll go back?

I don't know.

Henry set his plate on the floor, in front of Jacque's snout. Jacques devoured the leftover food, and then began to fastidiously lick the plate with his blubbery tongue.

Henry looked at Piers, who seemed to be adrift in thought.

If you don't mind my asking. . . the thing that happened to your arm, is that, is that why you left L.A?

The thing that happened to my arm, Piers responded softly, quizzically, having forgotten the lie she had told Henry, then remembering, emboldening her tone—Yea, the thing that happened to my arm. I guess you could say that's why I left, it was—

Piers paused, switched gears

—But no, not really. No. No one did this to my arm. It just sort of happened. On its own.

So no one got rough with you?

No, but—just no.

Henry nodded and Piers kept shaking her head, as if sanctifying the closure of her no.

Now it's my turn for the interrogation, Piers crackled. What's up with you and Gwen?

Me and Gwen? What do you mean, what's up? Nothing's up.

Oh no? Then why is your face turning red?

A look splashed across Henry's face and Piers thought it could morph into anger and explode, but it softened and dissolved into sheepish resignation.

Gwen is great—

She's hot, like, older-woman hot—

Henry laughed.

Yea I guess you could say that, older-woman hot. . . how old do you think Gwen is?

Piers pursed her lips and knitted her brows.

Fifty?

That's really good. She's turning fifty next month.

Fifty and she's still got it. Elizabeth Starling lives.

Henry and Piers shared in a laugh.

So she's 50 and you're like, what, 55?

53.

53. There you go, you could've been in junior high together. Were you?

No, she was in L.A. Elizabeth Starling, remember? And what about you, how old are you? Really?

I'm 21, Piers smiled. That's what it says on my I.D.

Yea, but what would it would say on your birth certificate?

Piers hesitated, then offered—It would say: Pierangela Grace Lucener, November 27th, 1972.

Henry quickly did the math in his head.

So that would make you seventeen?

Ssssshhhh, but don't tell anyone, Piers whispered.

There's an old Navy saying I learned from my father: Loose lips sinks ships. So don't worry, your secret's safe with me.

Piers bowed her head in gratitude.

Fortune cookie, Henry held one out to her.

Yea, thanks, Piers took it and unwrapped it. She snapped it into halves, ate one half and then the other, then read her fortune to herself.

Well, what does it say, Henry pressed.

'Remember this date three months from today'. Hmmm. Wonder if that's auspicious or ominous?

What does auspicious mean, Henry asked.

Promising.

Go with auspicious then.

And your fortune Mister Hook?

Henry cracked open his cookie and fished out the fortune.

It's blank, Henry said.

Really? Let me see.

Henry handed her the slip of paper and Piers confirmed—It *is* blank. I think you might be the first person in the history of fortune cookies to get a blank fortune.

Henry smiled—Wonder if that's auspicious or ominous?

Go with auspicious, Piers handed the fortune back to Henry. You gonna eat your crumbled cookie?

It's all yours, Henry swept the sugary fragments toward Piers.

Henry stretched his arms overhead and bellowed a yawn—Time for a smoke.

And one of your records?

Henry grinned—Yea and one of my records.

It was one of Henry's evening rituals. Sitting on the couch, smoking, and listening to records. His collection mostly comprised Irish music, folk songs, and ballads. His favorite singer was the operatic Irish tenor, John McCormack.

As Henry selected a McCormack record from his collection, Piers cleaned up in the kitchen. Then she covertly grabbed a vial and cloth from her backpack and went into the bathroom to huff.

Henry placed an album on the turntable, set the needle, the wooly crackle of audio-lint.

Henry sat down on the couch, lit a cigarette, and reclined.

Piers came back and sat on the carpet, braced against the edge of the couch.

She took in McCormack's magisterial voice, round and silvery. It swelled and deflated, brightened and dimmed.

Behind the lyrics and notes, Piers grazed the texture of an old-fashioned facsimile of Heaven. It was the Heaven of technicolor and fairgrounds and plaster saints, of waltzing sweethearts and theatrical grieving.

She allowed herself to go there, and there she was a different person.

She was a starlet with a glossy poster for a face, she was a young girl with white flowers growing out of her hair, she was her mother in a blue evening gown, and then she was disgusted. She rejected this Heaven, and said to Henry, baring teeth in her voice—Why do you like this stuff?

Henry, who had been listening with eyes closed, was startled by Piers's voice, by the contempt sharpening it.

Why do I like it? Well I like it because, well, because it's beautiful. And powerful. Not to your taste?

Not to my taste, no. I don't know, it's so, I don't know, never mind. . . I don't wanna ruin it for you, so I'll just shut up and listen to my Walkman.

Piers got up and retrieved her Walkman from her coat. She went through her backpack and picked out a cassette. Nine Inch Nails *Pretty Hate Machine.*

She slid the cassette into the Walkman, placed the headphones over her ears, and lay on the floor, head propped on her backpack.

She listened to her music, eyes open, mouth occasionally twitching a lip-sync.

Henry looked at her, at her bad arm.

Who is she running away from, he wondered.

And what kind of drugs is she on?

Henry tried to put it out of his mind.

He stubbed out his cigarette in the ashtray and immediately lit another one.

He closed his eyes, allowing McCormack's goldsilk rendering of "Angels Guard Thee" to move through him:

Awake not yet from thy repose,
A fair dream spent hovers near thee,
Weaving a web of gold and rose,
Through dreamland's happy isles to bear thee.
Sleep, love, it is not yet the dawn,
Angels guard thee, sweet love, till morn

This, while Piers absorbed the cyborg seething of NIN's "Terrible Lie":

Hey God
I really don't know what you mean
Seems like salvation comes only in our dreams
I feel my hatred grow all the more extreme
Hey God
Can this world really be as sad as it seems?

Lying on the carpet,
between Henry and Piers,
Jacques was asleep,
snout cradled in his crossed paws,
dreaming dog dreams.

Peekaboo, 1988

(A Deleon project inspired by the 1941 film *I Wanted Wings*)

I Wanted Wings is an aviation drama starring William Holden and Ray Milland, with a nineteen-year-old Veronica Lake in her breakthrough role as the sultry lounge singer Sally Vaugan. *I Wanted Wings* was the film in which "Veronica Lake", who had appeared in five previous films under the name Constance Keane, (and whose full birth name was Constance Marie Frances Ockelman,) was born. This happened in two ways:

1) Arthur Hornblow, the producer of *I Wanted Wings*, wanted Constance to change her name. "Lake", because her icy blue eyes were lake-like, and "Veronica," which suggested classic beauty, or maybe even a trace of its Ecclesiastical Latin roots to the phrase *vera icon*, meaning "true image".

2) Lake's trademark peekaboo hairstyle was serendipitously spawned during her audition for the film when, according to Miss Lake: "My hair kept falling over one eye and I kept brushing it back. I thought I had ruined my chance for the role. But Hornblow was jubilant about the eye-hiding trick. An experienced showman, he knew that the hairstyle was something people would talk about."

Interestingly, Veronica Lake's hair, which became all the rage in the 1940s, also became a tool of patriotism when the government asked her if she could change her hairstyle, thereby inspiring women working in war industry factories to adopt practical hairstyles that would decrease hair-caught-in-machinery-related accidents. Lake's honeyed locks were swept up and pinned back, a hairstyle change which coincided with the rapid descent of Lake's fiery star. As Miss Lake once proudly attested, "I will have one of the cleanest obits of any actress. I never did cheesecake. . . I just used my hair."

In Jayne Lockwoode's article "By Shear Accident, or How a Slip Can Lead to a Big Break" (Scintilla, May/June, 1982) she intentionally alters Lake's "eye-hiding-trick" to "I-hiding-trick". The essay continues examining the fortuitous origins of Lake's peekaboo bang and expanding upon an exposition on the role of identity in the female persona.

Constance Marie Frances Ockelman, a.k.a. Veronica Lake, a.k.a. the Peekaboo Girl, died on July 7th, 1973, at the age of fifty, from acute hepatitis and kidney failure brought on by years of alcohol abuse.

Peekaboo is filmed in 16mm black & white,
footage faintly graffitied with motes and spots and squiggles,
like peering through a glyphic window at dusk.

The interior of a nightclub.
The camera's eye frozen
on a lounge singer, from behind.
We see, in close-up, kinky tresses cascading over a sequin-studded evening gown.
Over the singer's right shoulder, in the near distance, a round table
occupied by two men, smoking.
Their faces are obscured, a couple of embryonic swabs, but we know they are
looking at and listening to the singer.
(Note #1: DeLeon cast Piers as the singer because, at 5'2, if that, she was of similar height and build to the 4'11 Veronica Lake.)
We hear a song being sung,

the slow-drip poison of snake-charm
filtered through blue smoke,
and that song is "Born to Love,"
originally lip-synced by Veronica Lake in *I Wanted Wings*.

(Note #2: The woman behind Veronica Lake's singing was
Martha Mears, a prolific dubber during the Golden Age of
Hollywood. Martha provided vocals for such luminaries as Claude
Colbert, Eva Gabor, and Rita Hayworth. In *Peekaboo*, Piers's
singing voice belonged to Trink, and one could speculate that
DeLeon chose to dub the vocals, not because Piers couldn't carry
the tune, but rather to mimic or pay homage to the Veronica Lake-
Martha Mears relationship.)

A voice, husky, tremulous,
maple syrup on steroids,
crooning:
My love
would be a lovely thing
how I cling
I was born to love

The camera smoothly glides over the shoulder of the singer,
who disappears from the shot,
and zooms in on two men sitting at the table.
They are handsome, young, dressed in suits. One has dark hair,
the other light hair.

Dark: They should put that on the menu. How'd you like to
meet her?
Light: Beat her?

Dark: Meet her, MEET her.

Light: Oh. No, no, no.

Dark: Yes, yes, yes. You wait here, I'll show you how it's done.

Cut to a close-up of the singer from the front.

A luxuriant sheaf of hair screens the right side of her face.

(Note #3: This is the only film in which Piers allowed DeLeon to film her from the front, and the only one to show her face.

Piers: I consented because I was wearing that blonde wig and half of my face was hidden behind the peekaboo.

DeLeon worked with Piers in perfecting what he called the "Lake-look," that ineffable quality of not-there-ness.)

The singer finishes singing, though the melody continues playing.

The shot expands to include Dark, who approaches the singer from her left.

Dark (extending his hand): Shall we?

Singer: Sorry but I don't dance with the customers.

Dark: If you dance with me, I'll put you in the Air Corps.

Singer: Thanks, but I don't think I'm the type for wings.

Dark: Oh, but I think you are.

Dark grabs her hand and the two of them begin whirling in a congenial haze,

a dance whose point of stability is not the floor but the camera.

Singer: Say, who are you?

(Dark whispers into her ear)

Singer: Now I know you're lying.

Dark: Oh yea? Why's that?

(Singer whispers into his ear)

Dark: Ah, I see. Well don't believe everything you read in the papers.

The camera glides away from the dancefloor to a nearby table, where a man and a woman are sitting.

The woman is soap-clean and lovely, the man frat-handsome and box-shouldered.

Man (bedwettingly excited): So it's fourth down, right, and we've got like ninety-eight yards to go for a touchdown. Should I play it safe and kick, or take a chance and run?

The woman is staring off dreamily.

Man: I said, should I kick or run—

Woman: Yes.

Man: Huh? Yes what? Kick or run?

Woman (making eye contact): How many men did you say were on base?

The man stares off in the direction where the woman was staring.

Man: You know, strictly speaking behind that guy's back, he's awfully conceited.

Woman (dreamy milktone matching the glaze in her eyes): Yes, isn't he?

Cut to a shot of Dark and Singer, Man and Woman, dancing next to each other.

The quartet slowly rotates in an elliptical orbit, a ceaseless, opiate spinning affecting a rhythm that dictates the flow of the conversation: who's saying what to whom and when.

(Panning Toward)
Woman: You sing beautifully, Miss. . . ?
Singer: Thank you.

(Panning Away)
Singer: Who's that making time with your girl?
Dark: That's. . . My girl? Who says she's my girl?
Singer: She does. With her eyes.
Dark (laughing): You're way off the course, you know that, right?
Singer: Am I?

(Toward)
Woman: It was a real pleasure listening to you. You have great talent.
Singer: You could put all the talent I had into my left eye and still not suffer from impaired vision. That's a quote.
Woman: By whom?

(Away)
Singer (hallway-voiced):
My love
would be a lovely thing
how I cling
for I was born to love

Dark: No, *you*, really?

(Toward)
Dark: Hey, Mack, wanna know something, this woman was
born to love.
Man: How do you know that?
Dark: She just sang so.

The camera withdraws and lingers on the dancers, the dance,
for about thirty seconds.
The vitreous creases overlaying the shot, the batshit patina, the
insistent flickering and wavering,
seems to be telling us, in no uncertain terms, that the film and
all the life it contained,
was dying or could die at any moment.

It was a warm, overcast afternoon. The wind was in a mercurial mood, vacillating between gentle and ornery. There was a charge in the air.

Piers was staked out across the street from the high school schoolyard. She was wearing her gray overcoat and blue hooded sweat-jacket beneath. The hood was pulled over her head. She leaned against a telephone pole and waited. She imagined that she looked like a stalker, and this lighted a smile inside her.

The schoolyard came alive during the lunch break. Piers took in the student-body, a bright noisy nucleus that dissimulated into factions. Some squalled invectives and put-downs. Some kicked soccer balls and shot hoops. Others pranked.

At one point, a boy, blubbery and squint-eyed, a killer whale with limited mobility, zeroed in on Piers and shouted through cupped hands—Hey, you fucking orphan, go find a cardboard box to roll up in.

The boy laughed his snarkwhale laugh, and the boys that flanked him cheered and hooted their approval.

At first Piers didn't respond. She remained poised and wondered—Do I look like an orphan?

This, like the stalker notion, lighted a smile inside her.

Then, on a delay, she unfurled a middle finger, prompting Whaleboy to snap—

Fuck you, you dirty hippy bitch, you fucking skank.

Piers held her middle finger, its architecture unflinching.

Psycho, was the last thing Whaleboy shouted before he turned and walked away, as did the rest of his posse.

Piers relented her middle finger. And immediately became grateful for the incident in that it had captivated the attention of a caramel-skinned girl with short dark hair and purple tortoiseshell glasses. The girl was staring at her and smiling.

Piers's heart jumped.

Not only because the girl was staring at her and smiling, but also because she reminded Piers of her childhood friend, Autumn.

Piers, needing to test the waters, removed her hood, revealing her head and face.

The girl kept smiling and gave a short wave.

Piers waved back.

Then she motioned for the girl to move toward the fence.

Piers crossed the street and met the girl at the fence, both on either side.

The girl furled her fingers around the webbed metal and leaned in—You smoke?

Weed?

Yea.

Sure.

You got some?

No.

Can you get some?

No. I'm not from here.

Oh. Where you from?

L.A.

Cool. I might be able to get some. You got any money?

Piers was close to broke but took a crumpled ten dollar bill out of her pocket and handed it to the girl through the fence.

Cool. You wanna meet me here after school?

Sure. When's that?

3:30.

What time is it now?

The girl scanned her wristwatch.

Almost one.

Okay, I'll be back at 3:30. I'll be across the street. By my telephone pole.

Piers smiled, as did the girl.

I like the way you handled Juan. That kid who was yelling at you. He's a douchebag.

He advertises it well.

The girl laughed, turned to leave and stopped—Also I like your shaved head. It's cool-looking.

Thanks.

Piers pressed her scalp against the fence.

Wanna touch it?

Maybe later, the girl smiled, then bolted.

Piers watched her until she disappeared into the brick building.

After-school, Piers found out the girl's name was Teresa, she was sixteen and Hispanic.

Teresa had scored a dime-bag. She took Piers to a place called the Ditch. It was an abandoned railroad track, slotted in a stubbly decline. It was where people, especially young people, went to hang out and drink and smoke and do other things.

Teresa guided Piers to a cylindrical tube, which functioned as a tunnel or bypass.

There they smoked, and Piers introduced Teresa to Sike.

Teresa's hysterical laughter morphed into a convulsive fit of weeping and then into panic.

Piers told her to lie down, it was okay, just lie down.

Teresa lay down on the cold metal and stared up at the scarred ceiling of the tube.

Piers lay down next to her.

Teresa stopped crying and then started again. She shivered.

I'm scared, Teresa whimpered.

Piers held her hand and told her that it was okay, that they had all the time in the world and they could lie like this and lie like this, it was okay, and Teresa enjoyed the soft quality of Piers's voice and began to feel better. She began to hum and glow, and Piers took off her coat and sweat-jacket and shirt and showed Teresa her angel-wings.

Teresa traced the angel-wings with her index. Despite the fact that they seemed to be made from ordinary dark ink, they felt feathery. And seemed to be breathing.

Teresa was amazed and got lost in their texture.

She traced and Piers shivered.

When Piers took off her pants, Teresa was moved to do the same, and the two girls massaged fire between each other's legs, and then Piers yielded her mouth to where Teresa was most burning, her tongue-stud a metallic tremolo, and Teresa's fire found its voice and rapture.

The Boy and the Warlock
by Pierangela

Once there was a beautiful boy with wings. His wings were also beautiful. Or maybe the boy was beautiful because of his wings. These were wings that some people could see, and some people could not but the boy knew he had them and he loved how they wrapped around him at night. It was a feathery hug that made him feel safe and warm. It was like sleeping next to an angel.

When the warlock came into the boy's life (the boy didn't know the warlock was a warlock until much later) he fed the boy apples. The apples tasted good but also not good. The warlock told the boy that the apples were good for him. Except the boy started getting sick and his wings started to fall apart. Every day more feathers fell out.

The boy was sure it was because of the apples and didn't want to eat them anymore but the warlock had grown stronger and the boy weaker and the warlock forced the boy to eat the bad apples.

The boy hoped he would choke to death on the apples before his wings disappeared completely. Except the boy didn't choke to death and his wings didn't disappear. Now when the boy slept at night there were no more feathery hugs. There was no angel in his bed.

The boy now felt lonely and sad and wanted to cry

but couldn't. The bad apples had taken away not only his wings but also his tears. And other things too.

The boy would lie awake at night and think of ways to destroy the warlock. And think and think.

The boy missed his wings dearly and wanted to cry for them but couldn't but knew he could make himself strong again because the trees in his yard were feeding him good apples. Golden apples.

The trees will feed me golden apples and I will grow strong and I will destroy the warlock once and for all and I will be able to say The End and not just dream it.

"The quality that we call beauty, however, must always grow from the realities of life, and our ancestors, forced to live in dark rooms, presently came to discover beauty in shadows, ultimately to guide shadows toward beauty's ends

—Jun'ichirō Tanizaki, *In Praise of Shadows*

"What's he going to do?"

"Nothing."

"They'll kill him."

"I guess they will."

"He must have got mixed up in something in Chicago."

"I guess so," said Nick.

"It's a hell of a thing."

"It's an awful thing," Nick said.

They did not say anything. George reached down for a towel and wiped the counter.

"I wonder what he did?" Nick said.

"Double-crossed somebody. That's what they kill them for."

"I'm going to get out of this town," Nick said.

"Yes," said George, "that's a good thing to do."

"I can't stand to think about him waiting in the room and knowing he's going to get it. It's too damned awful."

"Well," said George, "you'd better not think about it."

Joe closed the book and set it down.

He kept thinking about it.

What the "killers" were going to do to Ole "Swede" Anderson. And how in the film adaptations that thing was done but in the story it wasn't. You were left to keep thinking about it and it was to be continued off the pages, to be continued in your mind.

Joe rose from his bed, lit a cigarette, and paced. He looked out the window. The Hemingway story had had a polarizing effect on him. He felt relaxed and agitated, sedate and disturbed.

It was the first Hemingway story he had ever read. The first Hemingway anything he had ever read. Even though reading the story was not a mandatory part of the impending assignment, (he and Max were ordered to watch the 1946 and the 1964 film adaptations of *The Killers*) he had taken it upon himself to check out the source from which the films derived.

Joe had found a used copy of *The Short Stories of Ernest Hemingway* at a bookstore. He had looked inside and saw that someone had marked the copy. Passages were underlined in pencil, comments had been written in the margins. Joe liked that. He found it interesting to see what someone else thought of the stories, *how* they thought of them, and what they considered important enough to emphasize. On the inside cover, in vibrato handwriting, it read:

Hem themes: violence, fear, loneliness, alienation, disillusionment, trauma, hidden scars, insomnia

Hem's "Iceberg principle": the dignity of an iceberg is that 9/10ths of it lies underwater. Allowing the tip to suggest the unseen bulk of volume. He wanted to write like this.

Joe also found notes in the left-hand margin of the first page of "The Killers":

Originally pub. in Scribner's mag, 1927
Working title of the piece "The Matadors"
Written when Prohibition & organized crime were at peak
Seed: a story from Hem's highs school days
"A Matter of Colour" featuring a boxer named Swede

Joe also took pencil to page, underlining passages to get a feel for the cadence of Hemingway's style. The angular repetitions, the droning idiom, the jaded flatness of dimension.

He also made note of the fact that the term 'bright boy'

(including the conjugations 'bright boy's' or 'bright boys') appeared in the story twenty-nine times.

One afternoon, while eating lunch with Max at Jack-in-the-Box, he shared this tidbit with Max, who, with chewed-up burger clotting his speech, said—What's that supposed to mean?

It doesn't really mean anything. It's just a term that was used a lot, so I figured it was something we'd work into our dialogue when doing the job.

Bright boy, hah, Max smirked, his tone implying that he did not find the term altogether trustworthy or viable. He straw-sipped his Coke. Then—I can't remember if they said it in the films.

They did, Joe said, well they did in the 1946 version, but not twenty-nine times.

You counted?

No, but I remember.

What about the 1964 one?

They didn't say it at all.

Max was amused. He dabbed at his chin and mouth with a napkin.

You're a good student, Joe. Better than me. I mean, holy goddamn, you actually read the story.

It's a good story. You should read it.

Thanks, but no thanks, Joe. Me and words on the page don't get along.

Joe was going to tell Max how he had also dug up and listened to a 1949 radio play version of "The Killers", but he didn't want to come off as superior or boastful, so he said nothing.

Max, having just finished his burger, leaned back on his chair and hooked his thumbs into his belt. Buddha-like in his digestion pose and, as if on the sudden receiving end of enlightenment, said: So bright boy is one of our catchphrases, huh?

Max, unfortunately, would never have the chance to volley that catchphrase with Joe.

It was a week later when DeLeon informed Max that his services were no longer needed.

When a shocked and blindsided Max asked DeLeon as to the reason or reasons why, DeLeon launched into a systematic upbraiding.

Your efforts have become lackluster and your work ethic leaves a lot to be desired. The performance of your duties lacks depth and conviction, you're performing with a, a—

(there, DeLeon paused, and consulted an index card that was on his desk)

—with a rote void of vitality. Also, there is an inexorable streak of laziness in you that will always prevent you from engaging a role on the deepest level. Did you even read the story "The Killers?"

It wasn't, you didn't say that was required—

Exactly, Max, that's exactly what I'm talking about. You only give as much as is required of you and no more. You don't ever try and raise the bar.

When Max asked DeLeon for a chance to improve, to redeem himself, DeLeon said it was too late (sparing Max the knowledge that he had been grooming a second "Max" for a while now).

Joe, like Max, was shocked and blindsided when he found out about Max's dismissal. And the idea of pulling off the gig with a new Max made him feel awkward. You get used to someone. They had put in five years together as Joe and Max, and despite Max's occupational shortcomings, he thought they had made a pretty good team, that their banter had achieved a harmonious level of fluency. Yet Joe was also aware that everyone, including him, was expendable. The role of Joe, the persona, as much as he felt it belonged to him, that he was it, that Joe was him, despite all that he knew that if he didn't play his part with optimal skill and devotion, he would be replaced. "Joe" was a privilege, not an identity.

The new Max, or Max #2, was also portly, as Max #1 had been (it seemed the fat-skinny contrast was essential in DeLeon's casting). Yet Max #2 possessed an agility of mind that Max #1 either didn't possess or hadn't taken the time to develop.

Max devoured as much as he could in a short span of time, learning to play Max to the hilt: a whirlwind of acting lessons, a crash-course in classic noir and gangster films, and not only had he watched the 1946 and 1964 films (as well as read the story and listened to the radio play), but he also turned up a 1965 film school version of *The Killers*, co-directed by Andrei Tarkovsky and two of his classmates.

Max shared this version with Joe and DeLeon, both of whom had never seen it, and DeLeon found the "whistling" that came from the customer played by Tarkovsky a perfect melodious counterpoint to the taut menace of the scene,

i.e. a songbird's serenade at the gallows, and told Joe and Max that they should incorporate whistling into their characterization when pulling off the job.

It was a warm windless spring day when Joe and Max left for Redline.

One night, Henry introduced Piers to his rowboat.

Located about twenty miles from his trailer, the rowboat was a climate-scarred anomaly docked on a desolate plot of mesa.

You leave it here all year round?

Henry nodded—It's been in the same spot for almost three years.

The rowboat was encircled by tufts of sage and chamisa and an ancient arthritic tree was stooped over it.

Aren't you worried someone's gonna steal it?

Nah, not really, Henry clutched the handle of an oar. One of the oars was stolen and somebody carved this on the side—

Henry rapped his knuckles against the crudely carved letters, which read—*Ibid.*

Henry climbed in and sat down. The bones of the boat creaked.

Piers slowly circled the rowboat, appraising it with curiosity and skepticism.

Why'd you put it out here?

I like it out here. It's quiet.

Yea, Piers agreed, and visually followed the thrust of the stern, which pointed toward curvaceous dunes in the distance.

You coming aboard?

Piers climbed into the rowboat and sat on the seat opposite Henry's.

She canned the interior, formerly a dark red that had mostly faded into bleary rose.

Piers looked out toward the dunes.

What do you do when you're out here?

Nothing really. I just sit here quietly. Think, don't think, whatever. Sometimes though I'm sure I can smell the sea, maybe the wind has carried its scent all the way from the coast or maybe it's the sea from the past when this place was underwater. Did you know that this whole region used to be underwater?

No.

It was. Way back when.

Henry inhaled deeply, as if trying to draw the memory of the sea into his lungs and heart. He exhaled.

It will be again. Someday.

Piers smiled—And then what, people will have to grow gills in order to survive?

Like Atlantis Part II?

Yea maybe, Henry smirked. That or build boats. Adapt or drown.

Piers traced the splintered anatomy of the oar.

Have you named it?

The rowboat?

Yea.

No.

It's important to name things. You should name her.

How do you know it's a her?

Aren't boats always women?

Mostly, but not always.

Piers ran her hand along a chafed edge.

This one's a she, Piers assured Henry.

Henry smiled—What should I name her?

It's important that *you* name her.

Alright let me think—

Betty, Lulu, Susan, Beatrice—

Wait hold on, I thought I was supposed to name her?

You are. I'm just throwing out suggestions. To get you in a naming mood.

Right, Henry nodded. And pursed his lips.

Elizabeth.

Piers's expression brightened—Elizabeth as in Elizabeth Starling?

No, Henry quickly countered. Elizabeth as in Elizabeth. There was Queen Elizabeth and Elizabeth Taylor and—

Elizabeth Starling.

Henry shook his head and laughed and then coughed and then spit.

You don't give up easy, do you?

No, I don't. We small ones have to stay fierce. Like tigers.

Henry patted the side of the rowboat—You hear that, Elizabeth? The small ones have to stay fierce like tigers.

Now that you've named her, you have to baptize her.

Oh, come on—

Really you have to, it's important. Don't you want your boat to be blessed?

Henry regarded Piers with quizzical amusement. And played along.

Okay what do I have to do?

You have to...

Piers leaned over the side of the boat and scooped up a handful of dirt.

Here, hold out your hands—

Piers dumped the dirt into Henry's cupped palms.

Now we have to...

Piers spit on the dirt.

Now you.

Henry hesitated then spit on the dirt, a frothy bubble mounting its dark.

Now you spread the dirt wherever you want and say something.

What do I say?

I don't know, something official-sounding, some kind of blessing.

I'm not good at that stuff. I'll spread the dirt and you say the blessing.

Okay.

Henry scattered the dirt as Piers intoned—Blessings upon you, Miss Elizabeth, may you and Henry voyage safely through the desert. How's that?

That's good, Henry wiped his hands on his pants. Then he tapped out a cigarette from its pack and lit up.

So Elizabeth has never ever moved from this spot?

Not since I put her here, no.

Have you ever thought about taking her out, like on a lake or something?

No, this is her spot. Right here under our gnarled tree.

Henry indicated their hunched neighbor with a waving of his cigarette.

Elizabeth and I have taken plenty of trips together, and we've done so without ever moving from this spot.

No, I know, but she's a rowboat—

She's not that kind of rowboat, Henry abruptly cut off Piers. You're too young to understand what I'm talking about.

Piers flinched, as if Henry had threatened to strike her.

Hey man fuck you, that's condescending—

Sorry

No, no, I mean really. Just cuz you park your rowboat out in the desert and it doesn't go anywhere doesn't make it profound or special or something—

I didn't say it did—

I mean it's a fucking rowboat—

Yea I know—

Meant for water—

Would you please just, could you please shut up? This is my spot, and I brought you here to . . . I didn't bring you here to tell me what I should be doing with my rowboat, this is my spot and you're fucking it all up with your talk, you're just fucking it all up.

Henry's mouth violently twitched. His fingers opened and closed opened and closed.

Alright man, this is *your* spot, and I don't wanna fuck up your head. I was just saying. . . I was just saying.

Henry collected himself. Stared out in the distance. Allowed the quiet to cushion and envelop him.

Piers got out of the rowboat.

Where you going?

Gonna take a walk. So you and Mizz Elizabeth can be alone.

Come on Piers, get back in the boat—

Hey, don't fucking tell me what to do, Piers snapped. Don't tell me.

Piers's eyes pooled with fire. She felt it in her hand too. The good one. She couldn't feel anything in the bad one. The bad one had become impervious to heat and cold and to other things.

She turned away and began walking.

Moon-frosted mesa lay before her, a landscape with no conscience.

She walked, and she kept walking.

She ached for Sike, which she had run out of two days earlier.

The line clawed at her—*out of Sike, out of mind*—and she clawed back by laughing abrasively.

She collected stones as she walked and stuffed them into her coat-pockets.

Twenty minutes later, she returned to the rowboat and climbed in.

She dumped the stones, nearly two dozen, from her coat-pockets.

Piers picked up a stone and hurled it. Then she picked up another stone and did the same.

She held out a stone to Henry—Care to join me?

Henry flung the stone and watched it kick up dirt.

Do you ever pretend that you are out on the water with Elizabeth?

Yea, sometimes, Henry chucked another stone.

Well, let's pretend we're skipping stones on a lake, okay?

Okay.

Piers threw, and then Henry threw.

Piers watched the water spray jagged white teeth as the stones cleaved the surface of the lake. She narrated what she saw and said to Henry—Do you see what I'm talking about?

Yea, Henry lied, I see it.

It was a lie rooted in desire, in wishful visioning.

When they were done throwing stones Henry and Piers talked, emptied of residual animosity. Mostly it was Piers who talked, about puppetry, while Henry sat and smoked and listened. She talked a happy blur that eventually sharpened into inspiration.

Hey, you wanna see a show?

Now?

Yea, now. I'll do a show for you. No puppets. Just shadow-play—

She looked over the edge of the boat

—With the landscape as the screen.

Piers raised her hand and waggled it.

The never before attempted one-handed shadow show.

Wow, I'm honored—

You should be, Piers winked. What you need to do is turn on your headlights and angle your truck so the lights come over the boat.

Henry did this, generating a cylindrical trajectory of back-lighting.

Piers stood in front of the rowboat, a little off to the side, and tested the resolution by conjuring a series of shadow creatures: Rabbit, Cat, Spider, Snake, Pterodactyl.

That'll do, she said, then turned to Henry—So this is a story I learned from my mentor, Josef. It's a Japanese folk legend dating from, I think the 18ᵗʰ century. It's called *Okiku and the Nine Plates*. Ever heard of it?

Henry shook his head.

Well, there are different versions of the story, but all of them revolve around Okiku, a beautiful servant-girl who meets her tragic death in a well. In some versions she commits suicide, in others she's murdered.

Piers paused, deep inhale, emphatic exhale.

Anyways enough from me, let the shadows tell the story.

Piers begins whistling,

a dry, chapped wind,

the tubercular wings of a secret.

It stirs and it stirs

and then her voice, thin, whittled, somber—

There once lived a beautiful young maid named Okiku, who worked for the samurai, Tessan Aoyama, at the Himeji Manor.

Okiku appeared,
supple and wavering,
an amorphous hint
upon the earthen sheaf
of white fire.

Henry was instantly riveted.
She struck him as an entity
that had been fashioned out
of thin, night air,
and he eased into the story
as one would a sedative or warm bath.

He watched as Okiku rejected Aoyama's advances,

followed by the jilted samurai's devious plot to blackmail Okiku into becoming his mistress.

Ten rare and valuable golden plates, one which Aoyama hid, before accusing

Okiku of having stolen the plate.

Okiku, seized with panic, counted the plates: 1, 2, 3, 4, 5, 6, 7, 8, 9,

No, she cried, and recounted the plates, again and again.

If she agreed to become his mistress, Aoyama would grant her a pardon

and spare her the torture and execution which was the punishment for such a crime.

Okiku declined and cast herself into the well outside the manor and drowned.

It was then that her second story began, her legend.

Every night Okiku's ghost emerged from the well

and could be heard counting: 1, 2, 3, 4, 5, 6, 7, 8, 9,

before breaking into an unearthly scream.

The scream tore through Henry as if it had teeth.

He quickly lit a cigarette and was surprised to find his hand was shaking.

He waited for the story to go on, for Piers to say or show something more, but she didn't.

It ended unfinished, the scream binding the story and the silence holding it captive.

Henry looked at Piers who was staring mutely into the frosted pool of light.

He wondered how she had done what she had done and only with one hand.

And the scream, yes it had come from Piers, but she couldn't have been its sole source. There was something beyond just one girl in that scream.

Henry smoked quietly, waiting for Piers to return from wherever she had gone. When he sensed a shift, he asked—What happened to Aoyama?

Piers stared at Henry with vacant intensity.

He went insane from listening to the same thing night after night. 1, 2, 3, 4, 5, 6, 7, 8, 9, and then the scream.

Piers smiled. It was a smile carved from small victories, from vindication.

Fucker got his comeuppance, didn't he?

Yea, Henry agreed, unsure as to why he felt warm shame nesting in the back of his throat.

While the exact origins of the Okiku legend are unclear, it was first performed as a bunraku puppet show in July 1741 at the

Toyotakeza theater, under the title *Banchō Sarayashiki* ("The Plate Mansion at Banchō").

In this version, the Shogun of Himeji Castle has fallen gravely ill, and his heir plans on gifting him ten valuable plates to ensure his succession to the throne. The Shogun's chief retainer, Tetsuza Asayama, devises a plot which involves Okiku, the beautiful maiden to whom the heir is engaged. Asayama steals one of the plates and calls upon Okiku to deliver the plates to his chamber, where he attempts, unsuccessfully, to seduce her. Angered by her rejection, he accuses her of stealing the plate, but promises to clear her name if she agrees to become his mistress. Okiku refuses and Asayama beats her with his sword before suspending her over the well outside the castle and tortures her, demanding that she become his mistress and help him kill her lover. Okiku never accedes and is eventually murdered and cast down into the well. Interestingly, in this version when Okiku's ghost rises to confront Asayama, his response is not one of fear or disturbance, the play ends with Asayama gazing upon Okiku's ghost with contempt and disdain.

There are countless variations on this story: in one, it is the wife of the Aoyama/Asayama character, who breaks the plate and blames it on Okiku; in another, Okiku actually breaks the plate and is murdered by her master and thrown into the well; and one version with a liberating post-script has the Aoyama family hiring a friend to hide by the well. When Okiku's ghost gets to nine he shouts Ten, thereby freeing the ghost from her eternal torment.

The legend of Okiku is also a popular subject for ukiyo-e ("images of the floating world") artists, with the following woodblock print from the series *One Hundred Tales*, one of its renowned interpretations:

Hokusai, "The Manor's Dishes," 1830

Wriggling above
the jagged rim of the wooden well,
a spectral Gorgon worm, Okiku,
cortege unto herself, moon-carved
face a floating monument in the blue-black
night, she counts nine through
eternity, and her last measure,
a haunted tenth, birthing a scream
raveled in smoke, wafting toward Heaven,
a rumor, a dirge, a plea,
the tattle of bones.

In the late eighteenth century, old wells in Japan were infested with a type of worm known as Okiku-mushi ("Okiku bug"). This worm, corseted in thin threads, was believed to be a reincarnation of Okiku.

Himeji Castle, a.k.a., White Heron Castle (due to its pale white exterior) is one of Japan's most popular tourist destinations, where people can visit what is alleged to be the real "Okiku's well." Her haunt, like her scream, continues to echo between worlds.

(Newspaper clipping pasted into Piers's Journal, Undated)

Los Angeles Times, October 17th, 1987

The Day Live Television News Coverage Was Born

by Evelyn DeWolfe

They called it television's "baptism of fire".

The event that would prove television's power to communicate, that held its audience in the grip of the first major news coverage in the medium's history, focused on tiny Kathy Fiscus of San Marino, a blond 3-year-old who, on a footrace with playmates, fell into a 110-foot abandoned well shaft only 14 inches in diameter.

That unforgettable day was Friday, April 9, 1949. It was the day live television-news coverage was born.

Now, 38 years later, television viewers have been caught up in another rescue attempt, as workers inched their way toward 18-month-old Jessica McClure, trapped 22 feet down in an abandoned well in Midland, Tex.

The historic 27 1/2-hour telecast on KTLA Channel 5 of the Fiscus rescue attempt had such a profound impact on its viewers that those of us who watched the drama unfold still remember the almost unbearable agony it engendered in each of us as we prayed that

little   Kathy,   wedged   in   her   rusty
cylindrical prison, 94 feet below, would be
freed. But she died before anyone could get
to her.

(Piers's comments written below the clipping)
It makes perfect sense that live television coverage
would be born on the day a little girl died in a well.
Baptism by media storm.
What they <u>don't</u> know is that the camera existed
long before it was invented. And that what they
broadcast is seen not only by a living audience
but also by a dead one, images moving between worlds.
Like death wish fish vaulting from sea
to gulp at the sky, to kiss it.

"Where is the *duende*? Through the empty archway a wind of the spirit enters, blowing insistently over the heads of the dead, in search of new landscapes and unknown accents: a wind with the odour of a child's saliva, crushed grass, and medusa's veil, announcing the endless baptism of freshly created things."

—Federico Garcia Lorca, "Theory and Play of the *Duende*"

Piers's Journal, May 5th, 1984

Today it was blueberry pie and peach schnapps for the Two Calamities.

Me and Autumn ditched school and rode our bikes to the woods where we brought pie like we always do (me lifting it from the store) and I wonder how many pies we've eaten over the past 3 months. And we got lucky cuz Autumn's cousin Cody who works at a liquor store gave us four free shooters of peach schnapps.

Like I always do, I looked ahead in looking back and remembered those days with sweetness—playing hooky, eating pies straight outta the tin with our hands, getting buzzed on liquor—good times.

Those were the days, I tell Autumn while they're still happening, while we're in them, and she calls me crazy white girl cuz I talk like we're already old or already dead, not like the pie and liquor thing happened twenty minutes earlier, and she calls me crazy white girl cuz the Lakota used to call Calamity Jane crazy white woman and Calamity Jane is one of my heroes, Autumn's too, which is why we're the Two Calamities

We read a little from Calamity Jane's letters to her daughter, which Autumn gave to me as a gift (I love that it was put out by a press called Shameless Hussy) and later I brush Autumn's hair, it is long and dark and beautiful, and brushing it is one of my favorite things to do. When I am brushing her hair, I tell her I plan to visit the old man in the cave and she calls me crazy white girl and then asks why. I told her:

A) I want to see him with my own two eyes

B) people in town call him a weirdo and freak and I'm a weirdo and freak and maybe we're the same kind of weirdo and freak and we'll get along real well, and

C) cuz it's the Calamity thing to do.

When I asked Autumn if she wanted to go with me she said Thanks but no thanks, and then she asked me when I was going and I said in a few days, then she said Maybe, let me think about it.

And today I learned something from Autumn, a word I had never heard before. Axis Mundi.

She told me her people considered the Black Hills an Axis Mundi, which is a center-point betw. Heaven and Earth. She said it was kind of like a sacred bellybutton. I thought that was cool and was pretty sure I wouldn't have learned that in school (another good reason for playing hooky). When Autumn said center-point I thought of the time Uncle Clark took me to that spot just outside town, kind of in the middle of nowhere, and there was a rusty sign on a wooden fence that said—The Center of the Nation. Clark was proud and said Ain't that something we're at the very center and I said Yea but felt nothing inside. When Autumn told me about Axis Mundi, I did feel something inside. Kind of a warm tugging. Is that because it was Autumn telling me and not Clark? Or was it something else?

After I brushed Autumn's hair I braided it and told her how one day I was gonna cut off all my hair and she called me crazy white girl and also called me heyoka girl cuz I was backwards-acting. I like when she calls me that and crazy white girl, too. Even though Autumn is half-white, her Mom's white, she doesn't relate to that part of herself or hates that white runs in her veins cuz of the stories she's heard (really overheard) from her father and uncles and grandfather who call S.D. Indian-hating land. I can tell that their hurt is her hurt and when she tells me the stories I feel ashamed and angry and don't know what to say and usually say nothing. I hold her hand or brush her hair. Sometimes I braid it and wish we were sisters and that I had hair like hers.

Xerox of the first page of *Calamity Jane's letters to her daughter*, by Jane Canary Hickok, pasted into Piers's Journal, undated

Jim O' Neil – Please give this album to my daughter, Janey Hickok, after my death
Jane Hickok

Sept. 25, 77
Deadwood, Tery Dk.

My Dear – this isn't intended for a diary and it may even happen this will never be sent to you but i like to think of you reading it someday page by page in the years to come after I am gone. I would like to hear you laugh when you look at these pictures of meself. I am alone in my shack to night and tired. I rode 60 miles yesterday to the post office and returned home to night this is your birthday and you are 4 years old today. You see your Daddy Jim promised he would always get a letter to me on your birth day each year. Was I glad to hear from him? He sent the tiny picture of you – you are the dead spit of Meself at your age and as I gaze on your little photo to night I stop as I kiss you and then remembering tears start and I ask god to let me make amend somehow some day to your father and you. I visited

your father's grave this morning at
Ingleside. They are talking of moving his
coffin to Mount Moriah Cemetery in Deadwood.
A year and a few weeks have passed since he
was killed and it seems a century – without
either of you the years ahead look like a
lonely trail.

Tomorrow I am going down the Yellowstone
Valley just for Adventure and excitement.
The O'Neils changed your name to Jean Irene
but I call you Janey for Jane.

(Piers's comments written in pencil)

What is so fascinating is that no one knows

if Calamity Jane wrote this diary or if it's a work of fiction.

The woman who claimed to be her daughter (Jean "Jane"
Hickok McCormick)

came forward on a radio program in 1941 and said she was
the "lost" daughter of

Calamity and Wild Bill Hickok. She produced the diary to
back her claim.

Hmmm?

Did she write the diary because she so badly wanted to be the
offspring

of two Wild Western legends? Did someone else write the
diary? If so who and why?

Makes me think about my journals.

Are they real? Is what I'm putting down my real life or is it
something else? Am I just a ghostwriter? For who?

Maybe I should start keeping two different journals, a Real
one and an Invented one.

Would there even be a difference?

My name is Pierangela Grace Lucener, and I was born on November 27th, 1972.

That is a <u>fact</u>. And the beginning of fiction.

See what I mean?

Piers's Journal, July 4th, 1985

When they stand for the flag I know they are standing on a mountain of haunted bones.

This I know because Autumn has said so, and I trust her.

I read that the gypsies have a saying: bury me standing.

I cannot wait to leave here, to fly away over the bones.

Here Flies Piers:

(Roughly drawn
pencil sketch
of winged Piers
flying over graveyard
of bones & skulls
in some places
the page punctured
by pencil jabs &
nicks)

Autumn:

It's true, we used to hang around together a lot. We called ourselves the Two Calamities (laughs) We were hell-raisers back then, or we liked to think of ourselves as hell-raisers. Especially Piers.

We both had major issues with our families. There's a lot of alcoholism in my family, especially on my father's side, and Pier's Uncle Clark was a. . . just not a very nice man. Very cold, very domineering. I think he was resentful, or something, that he had to raise his wife's sister's daughter. His wife Sylvia, now she was a real sweetheart. Always helping people, always thinking of others. Unfortunately, she was under her husband's rule. He treated her like a doormat, Piers too, or he tried to treat Piers like a doormat, but you know she's not the type to be walked on without biting your foot (smiles) Piers used to talk about her aunt a lot, you know, her aunt died when she was nine, she died from cancer. . . once her aunt was out of the picture, I think things got really bad.

The last time I heard from her? Well, let's see. I think it was 1990 when I got this book in the mail from her, it was called "The Lowdown on Calamity Jane". It was written by Dora DuFran, she was this madam who ran a brothel in Belle Fourche back in the old days. They used to call her place Dinglin' Dora's. And Calamity Jane, at the end of her life, she worked at Dora's. She cooked and cleaned and did the laundry for the brothel girls. It was funny because Piers didn't include a letter or a note or anything, just the book, and on the inside cover she had written: We gave 'em hell because they raised us in fire (laughs)

Excuse me. . . .

(Autumn's youngest daughter, Keya, enters and asks her mother if she's almost done, to which Autumn responds—Yes, almost done, sweetie.

Keya props herself against her mother's knee, resting her head on her mother's lap and angling it sideways, and asks—Who you talking to?

Autumn smiles, whispers something into her daughter's ear, tugs on her earlobe and begins tickling the back of her neck, as Keya breaks into a giggle fit. Then Autumn lovingly pats her daughter on the bottom and says—Go tell your sister to start lunch, I'll be right there.

Keya says okay and reluctantly leaves.)

Yes, she's the baby of the family, she's three. She has two older sisters, Summer and Mika, and an older brother, Douglas. Anyways, that was the last time I heard from Piers. The well? (chuckles) Yes, I remember the well. We weren't friends back then, but she told me that story a number of times. And she never told it the same way twice. She had the true gift of the storyteller. The one thing that never changed—her chasing the white fox. You know, the Fox is a great teacher and helper. He's guided medicine men in finding valuable herbs. He shows you how to escape enemies and make your way through dangerous territory. He teaches courage under fire. There's a song from the Tokala Society of the Lakota, '*Tokala*' can be translated to 'Kit Fox', and the words are:

I am the fox
I am supposed to die
I already threw my life away
Something daring
Something dangerous
I wish to do

There is no doubt in my mind that Piers was chasing a white

fox, one with nine tails, that day. I'd say the fox called her to that well, to her destiny. She saw what she needed to see and acted how she was meant to act.

Crazy white girl, yea (laughs) That's what I used to call her.

Piers's Journal, April 15th, 1990

It was Gwen's 50th yesterday. There was a small party at Red's after they closed. I put on a puppet show using the new puppets I made. They're variations on the Hydra puppets, which allows me to play several different characters with a single puppet, and I've gotten pretty good at doing it with one hand. Guess my handicap has made me resourceful.

A couple of days ago I did a puppet show on the plaza at dusk. I did my Lion & the Mouse bit. There were about 14 or 15 people there and after the show, one of the moms who was there with her two kids came up to me asked me when I was gonna do another show and I said soon. It felt good to be working again for an audience and I even made a bit of money thru donations. And Teresa stopped by afterwards and we smoked some weed and fooled around. Teresa's nice and I like her, but I'm worried that she likes me too much. I'm pretty sure I was her first and she's kind of obsessed with me. Really-really wants to please me.

Grateful for weed cuz being Sikeless has fucked me up bigtime and fucked with my head. I've been all over the place, mentally and emotionally. My moods jump like demon jackrabbits. It's like everything feels not real and too real at the same time. Like how I thought Teresa was like Autumn, but she's not like Autumn. Maybe I wanted her to be like Autumn, like how it used to be, or something.

Gwen was real touched by the puppet show I did for her and she even got dressed up for the party. She was a real fox in her shiny green strapless number. I snuck looks at Henry sneaking looks at Gwen. He seemed to be enthralled by her shoulders and neck. Poor Henry. A little boy trapped in a man's body. And trapped there with a burning desire for Gwen.

Henry loves his rowboat

Henry loves his Gwen

but Henry's rowboat will not find water
and Henry's love will not find Gwen.

Just remembered that in my dream last night Henry was shot in the chest six times and killed. I saw it on TV. I saw it on a TV that was in a shop window, and after Henry was hit in the chest with the first bullet his face came alive with shock and he held out his hand like he was saying No-no-no, please don't shoot me again, but he was shot five more times and then he crumpled. I don't know who shot him. Then the dream shifted, and Henry's ghost was walking alongside me. I asked him if things were easier in the afterlife and he smiled like some kind of knowing Buddha and said No things aren't easier in the afterlife, in fact they're harder in some ways. I was troubled by this notion but Henry wasn't. And he said It's important to make what you want while you're here, you can make what you want to happen happen, you can make anything, and I was doubtful, but decided to give it a try, and that's when the dream ended.

I didn't tell Henry about the dream. I wonder if I should?

Right now, as I'm writing this, he's sitting on the couch listening to John McCormack. I have to admit: the fucking Irishman has grown on me.

By the bladed light
of a rotund silvery moon,
a coronary bauble,
Piers and Henry sat in the rowboat,
huddled in their coats
and the afterglow of the party
and sang

Row row row your boat
Gently down the stream
Merrily merrily merrily merrily
Life is but a dream

They repeated the song several times.
Piers mused aloud—You ever wonder about this song,
if it's like an existential nightmare or passive transcendence?
Henry said he didn't understand what she was saying.
Nevermind, Piers said, let's keep singing, and she introduced
an alternative verse.

Row row row your boat
Gently down the stream
If you see a crocodile
don't forget to scream

You know that one?
No, Henry said, but I do know this one.

Row row row your boat

Gently to the shore
If you see a lion
Don't forget to roar

I never heard that. Hey why don't you make up a verse?
No, I'm not good at making things up, you do it.

(Piers took a beat)

Row row row your boat
Gently down the drain
Ferally ferally ferally ferally
Life is clogged with pain

How's that?
That was good. You're a natural.
Thanks. Should we continue?
It's a long voyage, so yea. Singing helps the time go by.

Henry and Piers sang it again
and again, Piers inventing fourteen
verse variations along the way.

Joe pushed open the door and a bell sang.

Max followed Joe into Red's.

The men's dark hats and trench coats were beaded in snow.

Joe took off his hat and waved it profusely, air-drying the moisture that had accumulated on it. He put the hat back and surveyed the diner.

The place was empty except for two customers.

An old woman, wearing a green hat that fit her head like a woolen conch shell, was seated at a table in the far corner. Arms gelatinously splayed on either side of the table, she was hunched over her bowl as if divining messages from it. When Joe and Max entered, she raised her eyes and stared at them with listless gravity.

At the counter, which was lined with red vinyl stools, sat a rumpled, doughy-looking man with an eyepatch.

Snow in April, Joe piped, as if announcing the title of a hit song.

Snow in April, Max echoed, and began ceremoniously whistling a cheery melody, a tune belonging to summer and lazy Sundays.

Joe drew a yellow handkerchief from his coat-pocket and wiped at his nose.

Wasn't expecting snow, Joe continued in an amplified voice, obliquely directing his comment toward Henry and/or the old lady. Neither said a word.

Max kept on whistling.

The waitress, Agnes, who had been in the kitchen, came out carrying a plate of food, which she set before Henry.

Joe gave his nose one last thorough wipe—Something smell's good—and fixed his eyes on Agnes. She was a skinny thing, a vibrating twig with mouse-brown hair and blue eyes that dramatically projected from their sockets, giving her a look of perpetual alarm or eagerness.

Wanna sit at the counter, Joe asked Max.

Max stopped whistling—Counter sounds great—then resumed his bluebird melody.

These seats taken, Joe wryly indicated two stools to the left of Henry.

No, they're not taken, Henry said.

Joe sat down next to Henry and Max next to Joe.

Henry had almost expected to see these two men. Or two men like them. His nerves, high-strung to prophecy, had fretted the trouble. Was Piers at the trailer, he wondered.

Joe took off his gloves and laid them on the counter, one neatly on top of the other.

Max, who had ceased whistling, left his gloves on.

Joe folded his hands, ennobling politeness—May we have menus please?

Oh yea, of course, I'm sorry, I- yea, Agnes recovered from her nerve-inflamed space-out.

Henry watched as Agnes fumbled for two menus and set them in front of the men.

He wished it had been Gwen working and not Agnes. Gwen, constitutionally, was better equipped to handle situations of this nature.

Joe and Max scanned their menus.

Joe noticed Henry sneaking a look at his gloves, and issued a slashing side-glance—What's yours, brightboy?

What's mine? I don't understand.

That's what I thought, Joe puffed, as if he had won a small victory.

Then he turned to Max—What are you gonna order?

I don't know yet. What's brightboy over there having?

Both men's heads swiveled, nearly in sync, and Henry,

implicated by their gazes, flushed and froze, his fork hovering in mid-air.

What's that you're eating, brightboy, Joe pressed.

Bacon, eggs, home fries and toast.

Breakfast, huh? Well we didn't come here for no breakfast.

Henry stared down at his eggs, a little perplexed, a little ashamed.

You a regular breakfast guy, Max kept at him. Bacon, eggs, toast, round the clock, that your gig?

Henry was utterly mystified. Part of him wanted to burst out laughing. Part of him wanted to cry.

With Henry remaining quiet, the scene reached a tense impasse, which Agnes broke through—You guys should order, we're closing soon.

Closing?

Yes, we close at eight, Agnes's voice quavered.

Closing at eight huh? What time is it?

Max spotted a clock on the wall behind the counter.

It's 7:15, Max informed Joe.

More like 7:30, Agnes gently protested.

Joe looked at the clock.

According to my knowledge of time sister, when the big hand's on the 3 and the little hand's on the 7, that's 7:15. And that clock on the wall—

Is slow, Agnes cut in. It's about fifteen minutes slow.

Joe checked his watch: 6:26.

According to my watch, it's 6:26, but I'm still on West Coast time, which means… 7:26. About fifteen minutes slow, just like you said. Why don't you fix it? So it tells the right time?

We like that it's slow. It helps our shifts to go faster.

You hear that Max? It helps their shifts to go faster.

Time is the enemy of the impatient Joe.

Yea Max, time *is* the enemy of the impatient, exactly. You know this is a funny place, this diner. And this is a funny town. It's got a funny feel to it.

As soon as we rolled into town, Joe, I could feel it. That funny feel. The snow, the pink flamingo at the gas station, the dead coyote in the middle of the road, now the slow clock, and this guy here—

Max's thumb, a stubby Napoleon, indicted Henry.

Brightboy's also a funnyboy, ain't he? Ain't you?

A strange sensation passed over Henry. As if he had been in this situation before, a peripheral strain of déjà vu.

Without saying a word, he considered the butter knife set next to his plate as he also considered Joe's throat. Instead he raised his coffee cup to his lips.

We don't want no trouble, Agnes's voice cracked.

Heyyyy, Joe raised his hands in a gesture of innocence, we don't want no trouble either. We just want a meal.

Joe turned to check on the old lady. She was busy tearing up napkins and snowing their remains onto the table.

What's with the old lady, Joe asked Agnes. Is she out to lunch?

Max whistled the two-note cuckoo melody to underscore Joe's out-to-lunch assumption.

That's Wanda, Agnes said.

Wanda's just Wanda, Henry pitched in.

Wanda's just Wanda, Joe repeated to Max and smirked. Yep this is definitely a funny town, a real loonybin.

Yea, guess we can add 'Wanda's just Wanda' to our list of funny things.

Like a smug schoolboy Max counted off the funny things— There's the snow, the pink flamingo, the dead coyote, the slow clock, funnyboy-brightboy over here—

Mister Breakfast Pirate—

And 'Wanda's just Wanda'—

A place like this you can't make up.

Joe peered at Henry's burnt toast and asked Agnes—You got a cook in the kitchen?

A cook?

Yea, the person who makes the food, Joe rotated his hands as if attempting to rush Agnes into comprehension.

Yea, we have a cook—

Who's your cook, Max inquired.

Julio, his name's Julio—

Julio, Joe smiled at Max. Wonder if he's legal?

(Though Joe was not genuinely racist, he figured this line and it derogatory implication fit his character in the scene.)

What do you guys want, Henry braved.

Hey, listen to brightboy here, Joe said. I noticed a little edge in his tone.

Yea, me too, Max agreed. Maybe that's how he wound up a pirate. That your story, Captain Jack?

I have no story, I just wanna know—

We don't care what *you* wanna know, Joe abrasively cut Henry off while slamming his palm on the counter for effect. We care about what we wanna know, which is why we're here.

What my associate means by that, Max picked up the thread in a professional tone, is that we're here about a young girl goes by the name Piers. She's a little thing with a shaved head.

Have you seen her, Max's eyes pinned Agnes, whose eyes bailed to Henry's and then back to Max's—No.

You haven't huh?

That was an interesting hesitation, Joe noted. You sure you

haven't seen her?

Joe slid his hand inside his trench coat. It looked like he was pledging allegiance or gauging his heart rate.

I—I don't know—

You don't know what?

Hey guys, why don't you—

Hey funnyboy, why don't *you*? Okay?

Maybe funnyboy-brightboy knows a girl named Piers, Max pressed, a tiny thing with a shaved head, though it might not be shaved anymore, and she might not be using the name Piers so let's see. . . any tiny white girls roll into town in the last month or so?

Tiny white girl? I don't know anyone fitting that description. And I don't know anyone with a shaved head or anyone with the name. . . Pree. . . Preese—What was it again?

Piers, Max reminded Henry, then spelled it out in loud halting syncopation: P. . . I. . . E. . . R... S.

Joe turned to Wanda—What about you, Wanda just Wanda, you know anyone fitting that description?

Wanda, due to faulty hearing, lack of interest, or inner-space-voyaging, didn't acknowledge Joe and just kept snowing napkin confetti into her bowl.

Maybe the cook knows something, Max suggested.

No, Julio doesn't know anything, Agnes quickly countered. He doesn't speak much English.

Figures, Joe clipped, then popped an exhale. He slid his fedora to a higher angle and thumb-scratched his forehead.

Well, me and Max will be around, since finding this girl is of primary importance to us.

Why, Henry risked.

Why? Funny-bright wants to know why? He's the inquisitive type.

That's why he's funny-bright, cuz of his inquisitiveness.

Henry felt as if he were at the mercy of cardboard cut-outs, ones whose patter made him slightly tipsy.

Joe explained—Let's just say this girl did something she shouldn't have done… like remember in the old days when you'd ditch school and the truant officer would go looking for you? Well, me and Max here are like truant officers.

That's a good way of framing it, Joe—

Thanks, Max—

So as truant officers, with a responsibility to the public education system, we beseech you to do your duties as upstanding American citizens and help us locate the truant.

Max began air-bugling the Star-Spangled Banner.

Joe put his gloves on and rose from his stool—You should get that clock fixed.

Both men left without ordering, and with Max bugling the Star-Spangled Banner all the way out the door.

Joe and Max got back to where they were staying; the Land's Inn.

Max, complaining about a stiff neck and achy knees, decided to take advantage of the outdoor hot tub. Joe went straight to his room.

He kicked off his shoes and lay on the bed, smoking. The picture hanging on the wall, directly above the TV, was a diffuse watercolor of a cowboy on horseback, facing a rolling open range.

Guy's got a lot of breathing room, Joe thought, and recalled how he wanted to be a cowboy when he was a little boy. His dad had bought him a Winchester model B.B. rifle and he'd carry it with him everywhere. He had even named it, Shane, after his favorite movie cowboy.

Joe finished his cigarette, took off his "uniform," showered, and brushed his teeth. He popped two Alka-Seltzer into a glass of water and allowed the fizz to circulate before drinking it down in an extended sip. He filled the glass with more water and set the glass, along with another packet of Alka-Seltzer, on the nightstand next to his bed. For later.

Joe got into his bed with his Hemingway book. He clicked on the lamp and re-read the story he had read earlier in the day, "Hills Like White Elephants". He felt like nothing had happened in the story, there was nothing to it, and yet had been left with an odd, implacable sensation. It was as if Joe had been given a chicken bone to feed on and yet he somehow felt full. Was this Hemingway a magician?

After re-reading "Hills Like White Elephants" Joe moved on to "A Clean, Well-Lighted Place". This got him thinking about insomnia, which had plagued him since his early twenties. The story held a darkly tinted mirror up to insomnia and a need for refuge, and Joe saw an insomniac version of himself reflected in that mirror, his face rubbed raw with sleeplessness, a blanched void of a face that had been eroded by too many nights of too many nights.

Joe closed the book and set it down on the night-stand. He lit another cigarette. He began considering, perhaps for the first time, seriously considering, if it were time for a change. Was it time to yield his role, to give up the ghost of "Joe"? How much longer did he want to play this part?

Perhaps, Joe dryly reasoned with himself, I'm just going through a mid-life crisis? People go through mid-life crises all the time. It's normal.

Yet, instead of wanting to buy a motorcycle or wanting to make it with a younger woman, what he saw as common virility boosters, he wanted to drop his persona, which also happened to be his livelihood. Good-bye Joe and hello who?

Joe tore open the packet of Alka-Seltzers and plopped two

into the water. He drank the second glass slowly. He shut off the lamp to go to sleep but found, as he always did, that shutting off his mind wasn't going to come as easy.

Henry:

Yea, I suggested the badlands as a place for her to hideout. She wasn't into it at first, but then she agreed. I mean, I don't know how long those goons will stick around but they seemed like professionals and when she told me about what she had done and why they were after her, I figured they weren't gonna give up so easy.

She seems to think they don't wanna kill her but wanna do something worse, which is to cut off her hands. She said DeLeon was fucked up in that kind of way and he'd see cutting off her hands as fitting punishment.

Listening to her talk about DeLeon and Tabanid and Sike, it all sounded, I don't know, it sounded like some kind of scary fantasy world, some alternate reality or something. I feel bad for her. She seems pretty lost.

Yea, we're supposed to meet in six days at the entry gate and I'll update her on the goons and what's what. We did a Walmart run and I set her up with a tent, a sleeping bag, blankets, and plenty of food and water, so she should be fine out there.

Overview:
Through the cloudy and diffuse iris
of the camera-eye, we see,
from a great height and distance,
a slow-drifting speck, a blotted kernel
inching its way across the landscape.

A deliberate panoramic glide
unrolls the landscape
as if it were a weathered jigsaw scroll
set in relief.
It is geography modeling Mars and prehistory,
a geography that has converted its mirages and rage
into a muted stoicism, though its temper remains mercenary,
a scorpion's callous flick.

The camera, bearing conceit
and ceremony, lingers on the landscape
for a good long while, a controlled mounting
of tension and suspense, perhaps to prolong
the viewer's speculations on the speck—
who or what is it, where is it going, etc.,
perhaps to sanctify context,
perhaps an opiate stupor, a God-induced withdrawal,
or all or none of the above.

Whatever the cause,
the camera is obviously more

than a little in love with the landscape,
which, according to a previously cited text,
can be regarded as a "free-form sculpture
designed by a thousand Bedouin Michelangelos
with the patience of Job."

Much has been written, expressed, measured,
painted, raved and revered about this landscape,
yet the camera is content
to hold anonymous vigil
through all eternity
without saying a word.

"For instance, at a performance of Dr. Caligari the other day, a shadow shaped like a tadpole suddenly appeared at one corner of the screen. It swelled to an immense size, quivered, bulged, and sank back again into nonentity. For a moment it seemed to embody some monstrous diseased imagination of the lunatic's brain. For a moment, it seemed as if thought could be conveyed by a shape more effectively than by words. The monstrous, quivering tadpole seemed to be fear itself, and not the statement, 'I am afraid.' In fact, the shadow was accidental, and the effect unintentional. But if a shadow at a certain moment can suggest so much more than the actual gestures and words of men and women in a state of fear, it seems plain that the cinema has within its grasp innumerable symbols for emotions that have so far failed to find expression. Terror has, besides it ordinary forms, the shape of a tadpole; it burgeons, bulges, quivers, disappears. Anger is not merely rant and rhetoric, red faces and clenched fists. It is perhaps a black line wriggling upon a white sheet."

– Virginia Woolf, "The Movies and Reality," 1926

It arose in a blatant gust, an elemental fit of improv,

mating wind and dust and rocks and whatnot.

A dust devil or sand demon, as Piers's Aunt Sylvia used to call
them,

when she was young, if she and her friends saw one, they'd call
out

sand demon and sign the cross to ward off evil, it was habit,

and Piers, by rote virtue of her Aunt's standard, signed the
cross

and then followed the sand demon, which seemed to be in the
fevered grip

of rockabilly or disco as it gyrated about thirty feet

before the charged infatuation of dust and wind and sand and
rocks

dissolved and the sand demon was gone

its ephemera spanning exactly twenty-seven seconds

at 2:13, April 23rd, 1990.

The sand demon's abbreviated peregrination had led Piers to
the opening of a small cave.

Piers squinted and considered the fact of the cave, and the sand
demon's guidance.

Then she took her journal out of her backpack and scribbled
in the left-hand margin of a page

the epitaph of a sand demon

marking the mouth of a cave

. . . .

to be investigated

The cave from floor to roof was only about seven or eight feet, and those dimensions compressed further the deeper Piers went, and then she hit a passageway veering to the right which compacted into a tunnel, forcing her to bellycrawl with her backpack scraping the craggy overhead.

She advanced haltingly, having only one arm to use for momentum, her slingbound arm a dead weight that at least didn't cause her any pain.

She slowbreathed deeply the dark-flavored draft that respired in the tunnel,

the ghost-breath of ancient sea and old blood.

It got into Piers's eyes and nostrils and pores and she remembered what Henry had said about the whole region being underwater once upon a time and she also remembered

The sea is the sea
but it is also a sound recording of the sea
it is Memory shroud and fathomless
and freighted with echoes

Where had she heard that? From whom?
Piers couldn't recall the source
which she thought was funny and fitting since it was a passage pertaining to memory
and in not remembering she decided to attribute the words to Henry
though she knew it couldn't have been Henry
he didn't talk like that it wasn't his thing
Row, row, row your boat, that was his thing.
Her thing too.
Their thing.

And John balloonvoiced McCormack singing, (why couldn't she think of any McCormack lyrics) him singing, (she hummed snatches of melodies seeing if one would unlock accompanying lyrics) John mister goldenvoice McCormack singing

all sadness sinks to rest or glides into the past

yea, that was Henry's thing, too.

After an elliptical yet exhaustive scooching, the tunnel opened up onto a taller and wider chamber.

Piers reclined against a jutting rock and looked ahead.

A cleft of light poured in through a jigsaw aperture that was an exit back into the world.

Piers was in no rush to leave.

She closed her eyes and steadied her breathing.

It wasn't just sea filtering through the cave's breath, but also bowel-traces of earth.

Piers hadn't been in a cave since Josef's.

His cave, for almost two years, had served as her womb and refuge.

She recalled the time Autumn had visited the cave and how she and Josef had performed a puppet show for Autumn, the Legend of the Golem, and how afterwards the three of them ate hot dogs. Josef asked Autumn if she would share a Lakota story or myth, anything she'd like, but Autumn was too shy and Josef said that was alright, no pressure and later Autumn changed her mind and she told the Story of the Rabbits in which the Rabbit Nation believing they were too meek and powerless with no one or thing on earth fearing them, decided to drown themselves in the lake and were about to do so when they saw frogs jumping into the lake. Rabbit Nation's medicine man said there *is* a nation that fears us, it is the Frog Nation and because of the frogs, rabbits didn't commit mass suicide.

Autumn, who was my first love though she never knew it, or maybe she did

and we never kissed or anything, just held hands a lot and hugged and

slept next to each other and laughed all the time. Where was Autumn right now?

Piers, milking memory,
slow-filled her lungs with darksweating air,
and slipped her hand into her jeans between her legs
and gentled herself into frenzy
until she climaxed.
And then halfdozing she wondered

Is this what Adam and Eve felt like, outcasts in their own backyard?

Except Piers was Eve to no Adam or Adam to no Eve
or she was both Adam and Eve, a solitary twinning derived
from necessity
and want.

1. Piers was amazed by the breadth of modulations in which
    coyotes spoke and sang. Sometimes it seemed as if they
    were just outside her tent, and perhaps were. Other times,
    far-far away, as if ghosting their own echoes.

2. Dunes, like desert ice cream scoops,
    and hills striated in varying pastels,
    banded in vanilla ash.

3. Thin, craggy spires, which resembled calcified totems,
    protruding from the earth.
    Some were lean towering obelisks, others were shorter and
    denser, trunk-like.
    Piers assumed they housed faeries or similar entities.

4. Amidst staggering aridity and muted tones,
    scattered flares of yellow,
    the gilded expressions of tenacious flowers.

5. One night,
    a thunderstorm rolled in and raged.
    Piers, who had a molecular fear of thunder,
    was reduced to a fetally inverted five-yr-old,
    shivering and shaking and pleading
    for her mother, any mother,
    someone, please god.

6. Her favorite things
    were the Martian-red shards
    of earth-pottery that clinked when stepped on,

like glass being ground or churned.
She would close her eyes and
walk back and forth back and forth,
a sound bath that calmed her.

7. Is this what Adam and Eve felt like,
    outcasts in their own backyard?
    In this wasteland, would you just
    screw and screw and screw,
    the desperate conjugation of the lonely and the damned,
    trying to screw your way out of the desert blues
    and into a new reality atop the bones of Eden?

8. One morning, Piers awoke to a burning sensation in her
    crippled arm.
    After not having felt anything in that arm for quite some
    time,
    Piers was inspired to unbind the sling and confront the
    arm's rigidity.
    She managed, through an intense and sustained effort to
    move the arm,
    nearly passing out when doing so.
    She tracked the source of the rash to a row
    of red-rimmed lesions lining the underside of the arm.
    From the center of the lesions sprouted what looked
    like serrated nubs of steel wool.
    Piers smiled and then whelped fuckyea,
    believing these were the beginnings of her angelwings,
    or at least one angelwing.
    Piers lost track of time.

last night i dreamed of
my golem my other
why have you turned against me
i said / it said nothing
a formidable mass
a sclerotic fistbody
with waxwork skin
the color of twilight
even though we are standing apart i feel its weight
pressing upon me
as if gravity is working sideways like a battering
ram
whats happened to you
i ask / it says nothing
and it strikes me what to do
what it needs is me to embrace it
and that will melt its rigidity
dissolve its unfeelingness
i feel happy i have the answer
and how simple it is
i wrap my arms
around my golem and i feel nothing
which mirrors it feeling nothing
and then i understand
the golem is beyond embrace beyond love
it is too late
this makes me sad and i wanna cry
but because of the golem
its cold and distance
i cannot

There are no set paths
here, no marked trails.

Pinchfaced old man
khaki linen clothing
canvas hat
walkingstick
unsteady gait
whitedog
like earthcloud
bounding

Of course your mind plays tricks on you
there were no vultures perched on a rock
wearing straw boaters & polka dot bowties
performing a vaudeville death dance
of course not
but how funny would that be

(Piers recalling
how her uncle would watch
Abbot & Costello on
Sunday mornings)

1, 2, 3, 4, 5, 6, 7, 8, 9 ...

. . . .

What do you think Booboo?

Wow just wow.

Colossal indentations
in the earth.
If not Giant Rock People
then what?

Beneath the moonlight
brush-studded landscape
parched glowing shock of witches' hair

(Piers recalling
that Halloween
when she and Autumn
dressed as car accident victims
gashes blood gore
insides exposed
the whole bit)

the sense that i am always
just ahead
of someone
who is tracking me

. . . .

or that i am tracking someone
and always just behind?

Morning. A milkpooling of light
on pillars of salt.

Coffeecolored man in straw hat
leading his horse.
Man tips his hat
calls out something.
Piers ignores him
keeps walking.

Is this what Adam and Eve felt like?
Forsaken puppets & preymates
waiting for god knows what
and when?

(Piers recalling
brushing Autumn's hair
touching herself
there)

Again the coffeecolored
man with the straw hat
and horse
again he calls out something
again Piers ignores him.

Is he following me?

When we first met Trink
that day in Venice
I thought you were so pretty
& so cool and you felt like home
rightaway and I loved how you fell
in love so easy with people & things
your eyes would get all juicy & so so big
and you'd say you wanted to eat people up like flowers
that's how you put it you would like to swallow em whole
all their color & fragrance & form & whatnot
and your singingvoice was a flower or could be
but it could also be murder
or arson or don't fuck with me
your singingvoice could be & do that too
I miss hearing it miss our shows
and remember that one & only time
we hooked up and we laughed the whole time
like playmates getting it on
like sister & brother incesting just because
so silly
if you could see me now
wandering around badlands with Booboo and Jean
by the way my wings or wing is starting to come in
hallelujah
anyways can you imagine I went from
Knife in the Side South
Fucking Dakota
to La La Land
to the moon

or somebody's idea of the moon
except there's gravity

Trudging ahead,
void of context or direction.
And then she heard the music
but couldn't trust it
and then she saw them.

There were six of them and three were playing music.

Guitar, percussion, sax.

And as Piers drew nearer she saw that the woman playing sax had rabbitears,

poking up from her head like fuzzy pink antennas.

The vaudeville vultures with bowties were a mind trick, that she knew, but this wasn't, *they* weren't: these were six people, just several hundred feet away, three of them playing hard-driving jazz, the saxophonist sporting pink rabbitears, and yet Piers couldn't fully confirm the reality of her conviction until her presence was substantiated by the others, which happened when the music suddenly stopped and the guitarist called out—Hey there.

A friendly, inviting hey there.

Piers, desirous to affirm the sovereignty of her left arm, which despite its stiffness, was no longer locked and slingbound, laboriously raised it and waved.

The feeling of being *seen* by these people and being able to communicate with them using her left arm, generated a warm sense of crush in her chest.

The group comprised: Joseph (guitar), Rea (sax), James (percussion), and the non-players: Rose, Allen, and Peter.

There were two other groups (one of five, one of six) respectively doing their own thing in other parts of the badlands.

Seventeen total, this year's contingent of Edenites.

Joseph:

It was strange to see this girl in an overcoat coming toward us. It wasn't so strange to encounter other people out in the badlands, I've done the trip seven years in a row and have come across plenty of people hiking and exploring and all that. . . what was strange about seeing *her*. . . well, first off, it was dusk, one of those times of day when the veil is at its thinnest, ya know, and I'm half-gone playing music, and I look out and see this gray overcoat moving in our direction. . . that's what it looked like to me, a gray overcoat with *nobody* inside it (laughs). Yea, I was like what-the-fuck. . . Then it came closer and I saw there was a girl with short hair inside the overcoat. . . now that I think about it, you know what it kind of looked like, it looked like an overcoat that was sleepwalking (laughs).

Do I really think these badlands are the original location of Eden?

No, listen, you've got to understand, listen: I came up with the name Edenites as a sort of gag, to play around with the whole desert-in-paradise thing. I know there are a lot of people who think we're some kind of weird cult or neo-pagan-hippy outfit… hell, maybe we *are* a neo-pagan-hippy outfit, I don't know (laughs).

In all reality though, we're just a bunch of people who come to the badlands once a year for nine days and play music and talk and dance and pray and goof around and, we just enjoy each other's company and pay our respects to this amazing landscape.

I have no idea, nor would I claim to know, about the real location of Eden, but honestly, I think the external location is secondary to the internal one. We carry an imprint of Eden within us, it's always been there, it's never been lost, just buried. We've got to dig, ya know? Dig way down deep and find it and find other things, too, that are buried within us. It's all there. The entire eternal record. And if I'm wrong, I'm wrong. So be it. My buddy Paul always says—Things are too sacred to take seriously. I think that's as good a mantra as any, don't you?

Piers stared at the rabbitears and wondered. Were they novelty rabbitears attached to a band? Were they implants? Were they real ones growing out of her head? Wanting to respect mystery, Piers decided to not ask. She enjoyed the contrast of the neon-pinkness of the ears against Rea's glossy midnight hair and left it at that.

Rea and James now formed a duet. Joseph had sat down next to Piers, with the entire group encircling Rea and James at a moderate distance.

In preparing for the dark and the cold, several lanterns had been lit and blankets distributed. Joseph explained to Piers—Not sure if you know this but you're not allowed to have open fires here. People do it, but technically it's a no-no.

Piers nodded and double-wrapped herself in the quilt she had been given.

So you're camping, Joseph asked.

Yea.

How many days have you been here?

I'm not sure. Three, maybe. Four.

Joseph nodded, looked away briefly, turned back.

And you're here by yourself?

Yes. Well no, I'm here with Booboo and Jean.

Booboo and Jean, those your friends?

Yea. Wanna see em?

Piers took the yellow and red sock puppets out of her coat-pocket and held them up.

Tada! Booboo and Jean. My companions.

Joseph considered the sock puppets, and then Piers. And then he smiled.

I've come across different types of people in these badlands, but I think you're the first girl I've met traveling with sock puppets.

Piers slid Booboo onto her right hand and Booboo said—And this is the first time I've traveled through badlands and come across, what do you call yourselves again?

Edenites, Joseph smiled.

Edenites, yea, Booboo waggled her head sideways, so does that mean you practice Edenism?

You're a clever puppet, Joseph laughed. Yes, we practice rampant acts of Edenism.

Cool, was Boobo's parting word before Piers slipped her off and placed her back into the coat-pocket.

Piers tuned in to Rea and James, who were billowing toward a frenzy.

Rea, eyes closed, torqued and pivoted and wielded her horn like a brass saber slashing air.

A short, staccato conversation took place between horn and drum,

bright furls of idiom, before Rea spiraled off into her own freeform monologue.

A whorling zoobreak of sounds
rasped and grated and howled
and yelped and cooed and squawked,
mating calls pitched to rhapsody.
Rea's soliloquy of umbilical bop
took off in many directions at once,
a siege of kinks and ravels intersecting
and threatening to wreck but never doing so,
calligraphic precision allowing the music to skate on razors,
and Piers was magnetized by Rea's long hipless waist,
as Rea melted into a squat, wringing every last drop

of blood from phrases, and then she went down even further,

sending up frenzied Morse code on wings of gospel.

She blew benedictions. She blew hosannas.

She blew the largesse of her soul,

its graffiti and anomalies, through her horn.

Piers thought Rea would explode.

Thought she would finally see an actual person spontaneously combust

and would know why and how it happened,

a rabbiteared casualty of bop in the desert.

Yet on the cusp of what might have been her detonating point,

Rea pulled back and began to cool down.

Her monologue shed its animal timbre and eased into something softer,

candlelight in place of arson.

James whisked a subtle beat to stabilize and underscore the mood.

Wow that was intense, *she* was intense, Piers glowed.

Yea Rea is something else, she's on a whole other level, Joseph said. She's the protégé of Seldom Ran. Ever heard of him?

No.

Well, he is, he *was,* this world-class jazz saxophonist. He was on tour in Japan and he went to this nightclub in Tokyo and heard Rea play. She was twelve at the time. He told Rea and her parents that if she ever made it to the States he would love to be her mentor. Said she had one of the purest sounds he had ever heard come out a horn, and he had heard plenty. Anyways, when Rea was fifteen she received a scholarship to a music conservatory in San Francisco and Ran lived in North Beach, so he took her under his wing and became her mentor and honorary godfather. She did one year at the conservatory and then dropped out and went on tour with Ran. They did a bunch of tours together before he died in '85.

Piers took in what Joseph had said and nodded.

Once more she fixed her attention on Rea, who was caressing a ballad.

Strands of dark hair were matted to her forehead as a result of her earlier riot.

Piers liked that she was wearing tightfitting brick red pants.

It was a touch of fashion ill-fitted for pilgrimage in the desert, and this appealed to Piers's sense of what she called wrong-rights.

Neckties and camouflage, ballet in snowdrifts, vampire-bites in a bathroom stall, pink rabbit ears and brick red pants in the badlands, the very fact that she, Piers, existed as she did—these were things belong to the realm of wrong-rights.

Rea's ballad was almost done grieving.
It gently folded in on itself,
a wistful tapering, interrupted
by a bright atonal flourish, a self-contained fretting,
and then the clean fluttering fade
into silence.

The group applauded.

Rea smiled big and looked at James who gave her a thumbs-up. She gave him one back.

Then she pointed toward the sky and murmured something under her breath, before speaking aloud—Seldom always used to say—

And here Rea switched to a gravel-inflected baritone

—It don't matter none who is and isn't listening, Bunny, cuz the Universe has got the biggest ears and they everywhere and they always tuning in.

Amen to that, Allen clapped, which Peter echoed.

Rea sat down between Piers and Joseph.

Thank you, Piers said. You were extraordinary.

Thank you so much, Rea beamed through the smile which had remained a fixed constellation on her face.

You, darling, always make the badlands a badder and richer place, Joseph said.

Thanks baby, Rea leaned in and kissed Joseph on the lips.

Piers was needled by a twinge of jealousy. So Joseph and Rea were a couple? She had been hoping that maybe, just maybe, something could happen between her and Rea. Then again, something in her felt flimsy and enfeebled and she wasn't sure she could work up enough nerve to make a move.

Now that I've stopped playing, I'm so cold, Rea hugged herself and exaggerated a shiver as she sidled up to Joseph who squeezed an arm around her.

What's it like when you're playing?

What's it like? How do you mean?

I mean how does it feel, is it, what's it like for you?

Hmmm good question.

Rea thought about it. Thought some more. And then—When I was younger I used to imagine I was placing worry stones inside my horn and then I'd grind them up and blow them back out as fairy dust. I guess it's still like *that* for me.

The light coming off Rea's face was too much for Piers to face directly. Even though it hurt her eyes, it warmed her chest and stomach. She wasn't sure she had ever met anyone who exuded light with such an elemental force.

What about you, Pier…it's Piers, right—

Yea, Piers—

What brings you to these badlands?

Piers said she was visiting her uncle who lived in Redline and when he told her about the badlands she felt called to explore them.

Wow, that's amazing, Rea said. I don't think I'd have the guts to camp out here by myself.

Well, I do have Booboo and Jean, Piers produced the sock puppets.

Sock puppets, cool. Are you, do you work with puppets?

I do.

After having lied about her motives for coming to the badlands, Piers felt good about telling Rea an unqualified truth. There was something about that lighted face which made you feel bad if you lied to it.

Joseph and Rea were curious about her life as a puppeteer and asked questions. Piers began to place herself, to find grounding and renewal, in talking about her puppets and her role as a puppeteer. And both Joseph and Rea listened in a way that made Piers deeply heard.

When Piers asked Rea if, having grown up in Japan, she was familiar with the story of Okiku, Rea crackled—Ohmigod yes, yes, my grandmother told me that story when I was a little girl and I was *so* scared.

Who, or what is, 'Okiku', Joseph inquired.

Rea started to explain but Piers gently cut her off—Hey, wait, if you guys are into it I could do a shadow-show of Okiku.

Really, Rea's voice rose. That would be amazing. I've never seen it performed.

Well it would just be hand-shadows, but my mentor Joseph always used to say—

And here Piers mimicked the gravel-inflected baritone of Seldom Ran as voiced by Rea and applied it to Joseph, who in reality had a soft and clear voice

—Light, shadow, hands and imagination. That's all you ever need to conjure magic. Light, shadow, hands, imagination.

Rea clutched her stomach threw her head back laughed and laughed—Oh wow, you did Seldom's voice perfect, that was spot-on, you have a great ear—

Thanks, Bunny, spoke Seldom through Piers.

Bunny, Rea softly repeated, almost hurt by the word, warmed by it too, and Rea combed her knuckles along the length of her left rabbitear. Then she reached over to Piers and traced the outside edge of her right ear, as if needing to texturally confirm the difference between rabbitear and human ear.

Piers watched Rea's hand come into view as it retracted. She flushed with aching.

Joseph stood up and announced to the group that their special guest, Piers, a renowned a puppeteer, would be performing a shadow-play.

The circle collapsed into a cluster, facing Piers who arranged the lanterns accordingly.

Before starting she gauged the mobility of her left arm, which she hadn't used for puppeteering in over a month. Stiff but functional.

Upon lanternglazed earth
she performed the story
same as she had for Henry
expect now she had two hands
and in this version
Okiku wasn't murdered by Aoyama
but rather committed suicide by jumping into the well.

1, 2, 3, 4, 5, 6, 7, 8, 9,
and then the scream, which had a strange effect on Rea.

As if in a trance,
she picked up her sax
and blew softly into it,
notes
like dried petals
scattered in soft wind.

For the briefest of moments Piers and Rea met outside
themselves,
breached particles levitating toward union,
and then Piers returned to herself, as did Rea,
whose face had taken on a grave and ashen dimness.
Sombriety:
When one is suddenly wakened by grief, when Great Sadness
functions as both clarifier and humanizer.
It was a term Piers hade made up when she was younger.
Or had heard somewhere inside herself and repeated, the
vocabulary of echoes without.
Piers wanted to go over to Rea and kiss her and hug her and
touch her ears
but Joseph was already there, an arm coiled around her,
the two of them rocking to a private lullaby.

It grew later.
Allen and Peter retired to their tent.
Rea was now sitting with James and Rose. They were talking
about Greta Garbo, who had died a week earlier.

Joseph, who was exultantly riding the wave of a monologue about the metaphysical existence and location of Eden, with Piers his captive audience, suddenly stopped—You know what, hold on, I wanna show you something.

Joseph scrambled to his tent and quickly returned with staple-bound pages, which he handed to Piers.

You should read this. You could read it now, later, whatever. It's yours to keep.

What is it?

It's what you might call. . . a profound jest. For centuries satire has been efficient scalpel, maybe the most efficient scalpel in cutting through dried-up caca and getting at the heart of things.

Piers giggled.

What, Joseph smiled.

Nothing, just. . . dried up caca.

Piers giggled again. There was something about that term coming from the mouth of Joseph, who reminded her of a young grungestyle Abe Lincoln, that seemed wrong. Or rather wrong-right.

Piers looked down at the first page which had three words typewritten in the center of the page—The Lighted Fractal.

Did you write it?

No, not me, Joseph said. It was written by, well no one knows exactly who the author is, but it was put out by this group that circulates a lot of underground material and they go by lots of different names, mostly gag-names like:

The Bureau of Laundered Undergarments

Heaven's Diabetics

Dali's Llama Stash

They're modern kin to the Dadaists and Surrealists and. . . how *I* like to think of them. . . Pop-Gnostic. . . that's what I think they're doing. Gnostic thought and philosophies that are being contextualized for the world we live in.

Piers looked down at the title page again.

Then she looked up at Joseph, the dignified jawbone and boyish Honest Abe face—Do you know any Lincoln quotes?

Four score and seven years ago, Joseph orated on a beat and then laughed. How's that?

Got anything else?

Let me think, Joseph contemplatively rubbed at his goatee. All that I am, or hope to be, I owe to my angel mother. I think it was Lincoln who said that.

Piers reached for her pen and Joseph held out his hand—Wait, here's one more. Truly, I say to you, unless you become like little children, you will not enter the kingdom of heaven.

Lincoln said that?

No, Jesus. But it felt relevant. And it goes with the essay.

Piers scribbled both quotes at the bottom of the title page.

A short while later, after James and Rose had retired to their tent, Rea joined Piers and Joseph.

Rea laid her head on Joseph's shoulder and yawned. She asked Piers—Will you be staying with us tonight?

My tent is a little ways from here.

Well there's plenty of room in our tent if you didn't feel like making the trek back to yours, Joseph said.

Piers wondered if Joseph and Rea were implying a threesome. While she was more or less indifferent to the Joseph aspect of the triangle, she was excited about the possibility of touching and being touched by Rea.

Rea let out another big yawn—You should stay. No need to go wandering around in the dark.

Guess you're right, Piers agreed.

It's settled then, Joseph reached for a lantern and went to the tent, trailed by Rea, who was trailed by Piers.

Once inside the tent Joseph indicated the sleeping bag that Piers could use.

Then he and Rea cocooned themselves inside a single sleeping bag.

They both said goodnight to Piers.

Piers said goodnight and thanked them for sharing their tent.

Then she waited, heart beating rapidly, hoping they would say something else, hoping her suddenly intense desire for a threesome, for Rea's touch and smell and animal, would not go unfulfilled.

Piers's waiting was met by silence. She stared in the direction of Rea and Joseph, unable to make them out in the blackness, and after prolonged staring her vision adjusted and she could see their heads, with Rea's rabbitears extending like probes.

Piers resisted the urge to reach out and fondle the rabbitears, to feel their warmth, and instead placed her hand between her legs and quietly masturbated. She allowed her climax to rumble a quiet electric death in her chest.

Then she unzipped the tent and went outside with her sleeping bag.

The cold air jarred her.

She looked up.

The night sky appeared to her as a jewel-encrusted dome, opulence beyond measure.

She turned on a lantern, snuggled into her sleeping bag up to her chest, and read the pages Joseph had given her.

The Lighted Fractal

All that I am or hope to be I owe to my angel mother
—Lincoln as voiced by Joseph, April 1990

Truly I say to you, unless you become like little children, you will not enter the kingdom of heaven
—Jesus as voiced by Joseph, April 1990

Baby Jesus had a persecution complex before he was born.

Here's a weathered snapshot of the baby Jesus, supine in his crib.

Notice the charged alertness in the eyes, and his stubby arms and chubby legs modeling a phantom cross.

According to the testament of long forgotten prophet and sand-collector, Elijah Wilkes-Booth, Jesus's persecution complex preceded the womb. Or, as Wilkes-Booth so obfuscatingly penned: Messianic ships, burdened with the cargo of guilt and trespasses, always set sail from a beginningless center and arrive nowhere with prophetic regularity.

Though only a bite-sized sample, we begin to understand why Wilkes-Booth went from philosophical hotshot to trivia footnote.

Jesus was born. Whether it was a warm windless December day in Bethlehem, or a cold foggy August night in San Francisco, we do not know. Our parable is not concerned with region, zip code, dialect, exact time of arrival. Our parable is concerned with spirit.

Jesus's spirit, encoded with destiny, was a manic kaleidoscope, revealing cryptic messages and lyrics which he strongly felt but did not understand.

To everything turn, turn, turn. This is what it sounds like when doves cry. Row, row, row your boat. A Jew and a Roman walk into a synagogue.

Jesus, born into misunderstanding, was the original bi-polar and harbinger of paradoxes.

He felt love for all humankind, but anti-Semitism, couched in self-loathing, bristled in his gut.

He vowed to shut down all casinos, yet shot craps in the side alleys of the marketplace.

His inclination to turn the other cheek was matched by his desire to cast the first stone, and with a vengeance.

He'd gladly die for your sins, but would also attend the execution at which you were to be killed for his.

Then there was Jesus, the newsboy and barker, the street-singer and gate-keeper, the fox and the hound, calling out to anyone who would listen: "Truly, I say to you, unless you are converted and become like little children you will not enter the kingdom of heaven."

And all this before Jesus was five.

Jesus knew from an early age that the greatest battles he would ever fight would take place inside himself. And, consequently, the only victories he would ever gain would require abdication.

Jesus's battle flag was white. Not the white of defeat, but the white of conscious submission, of yielding. Also, an important yet often overlooked detail regarding Jesus's white flag was that it was blank. No symbols denoting allegiance, no team logo. The flag's lucid blankness allowed it to function as a perpetually clean slate, a token of forgiveness, an open canvas upon which others could doodle, sketch, paint, etc.

It was a white flag that stood for nothing and everything at the same time.

It was, according to Jesus biographer, Abigail Thurgood: One of the first unofficial emblems of democracy.

In extending the scope of Miss Thurgood's statement, we suggest that it was one of the first unofficial emblems of democracy *and* anarchy. Democracy and anarchy, not always viewed as harmonious bedmates, but like Jesus the subtle shifting of inner kaleidoscope will allow one to view things differently.

When we say Jesus, we also mean not Jesus. To echo an earlier statement: Our parable is concerned with spirit. Official signature, eye color, criminal record, marital status— none of these things matter to us.

Jesus, or Not Jesus, was a fresh miracle, same as Joe, growing out of the barstool at Fred's Tavern is a fresh miracle.

The raising of a blank white flag, coupling Democracy and Anarchy.

II.

Baby Jesus knew his future before he could crawl. It lived inside him like a wordless forecast.

If Baby Jesus had had language, he might have said—I am here to announce my candidacy for Crucifixion and Redemption. An election would only be an empty formality for my destiny was secured before I was born.

Or perhaps a word-engorged Baby Jesus might have suggested—Rejoice, and sing, and do not trust mirrors. For one man's reflection is another man's martyr. Or scapegoat. Or both.

Then of course there's Option C., in which a monosyllabic Baby Jesus, steeped in Zenimalism, utters a single profound word: Boo.

Yet as far as we know, Baby Jesus babbled, gurgled, burped, dribbled, and shit himself like any other baby. An exceptional spirit and destiny does not preclude one from the formative trials of infancy.

We have examined Jesus's early years, but what about Jesus the man, the messiah, the idol, and grunge icon?

My friend had a dream in which Sigmund Freud, or a dream-like facsimile of Sigmund Freud told him: Without Jesus, there would be no psychoanalysis.

At the risk of implicating my friend, and dream-Freud, let us widen that metaphorical umbrella to cover so much more. Without Jesus there would be no New York, no kosher delis, no Kubla Khan, no Christopher Columbus, no marriage and subsequent divorce, no armed forces, no Ritalin, no KKK, NRA or ABC, no hate crimes, no Martin Scorsese, or Woody Allen. Without Jesus there would be no Woody Allen films. Without Woody Allen there would still be Woody Allen films, but without Jesus, no.

Consider, one idol giving rise to an

elaborate network and wired collective of neuroses, complexes and disorders; a symphony of inner turmoil transcending time and space.

If you subscribe to this theory, then you will begin to understand why your child's aberrant behavior in class, or your husband's extra-marital affairs directly correlate to the once-upon-a-time existence of Jesus.

Are we saying Jesus is to blame? If Woody Allen is determined to put out one film every year, and some of those films lack depth and a sense of completeness, is that Jesus's fault? Well, yes and no, but mostly no.

Yes, because Jesus invented Woody Allen.

No, and mostly no because Woody Allen, despite being the brainchild of Jesus, has free will to do whatever he chooses. That freedom means he has the Jesus-given right to put out one film every year for as long as he likes. Same with your child's aberrant classroom behavior and husband's infidelity—these are, and here I bank upon the lyrics of French pop star and minor philosopher, Simone Lefleur:

The existential spinning of gears,
like clockwork,
like tears

And so Jesus, like ice cream, comes in many different flavors.

Throughout the ages "he" (who is really more of a genderless wind, an epic score, than a male or female) has appeared in many forms and incarnations.

At present, a wildly popular version of Jesus is the one featured in the Hollywood blockbuster: *No Cross Can Hold Me.*

As you can see in the following trailer, this Jesus is a He-man, zombie-barbarian, back from the dead to avenge the death of his Father (the film is set in a post-apocalyptic world where God has been knocked off and chaos and darkness reign supreme).

This Jesus, with rippling biceps and pectorals, a face road-mapped with scars, neck bearing a knotted tangle of blue-dark veins, eyes holding a volcanic fury yet leaving just enough room, a tiny lighted window, for compassion and perhaps grace, and palms pulsing with digitally enhanced stigmata, this Jesus is hell-bent on setting things right in the name of love.

The amount of blood on his hands, the number of severed heads staked on poles, all of that is secondary to the righteous restoration of the Good and Just.

Except, and here we refrain from offering up too many details out of respect for those who haven't seen the film, there is a climactic twist that turns the values of black and white inside out and redeems the dignity of gray.

III.

You have been handed a map. It is age-yellowed, its borders perforated, and bears the markings of finely sketched geographical dimensions. It is a map detailing a nameless region, or unknown island.

The hands that gave you the map are voiceless, so there is no information, history, or back-story provided. It is a map that is simply now in your possession, and you are to make of it what you will, or what you will not.

The map, according to esteemed neo-theologian, Archibald Clemency, *is* the treasure itself, and can be dug up in the backyards of one's own seemingly remote and faraway sense of existence.

According to Clemency, once the map is brought out of the dark and into the light, it will instantly incinerate, thereby freeing the map-holder from symbolic attachment.

Which brings us back to Jesus.

Jesus, when brought out of the dark and into the light, is burned to nothing, a vampire-style death by sunlight. Except, and here's the metaphysical kicker, it is not *nothing* nothing, it is a charged nothing—a glowing genome, a lighted fractal, a broken-off syllable seeking union with Word.

It is Glory-Be singing itself to rise,

the Phoenix scatting and be-bopping a shed through conscious arson,

a little girl crying her eyes out over her skinned knees

(and how Time scabs the little girl's wounds and dries her tears),

it is the mapless wanderlust and genius of love forever growing wild beyond names, facts, figures, history, and anything else equivalent to wet cement poured in a river.

Which is to say: Baby Jesus will be born tomorrow. Same as yesterday.

Or, to consolidate the mutable arc of our essay into a single shining passage, we present, for your appraisal, a time-tested gem carved by one Mr. William Shakespeare (who was also not William Shakespeare):

Tomorrow, tomorrow, and tomorrow,
Creeps in this petty pace from day to day,
To the last syllable of recorded time;
And all our yesterday's have lighted fools
the way to dusty death. Out, out brief
candle!
Life's but a walking shadow, a poor player
That struts and frets his hour upon the
stage,
And then is heard no more. It is a tale
Told by an idiot, full of sound and fury,
Signifying nothing.

Piers's Journal, April 1990

Tonight I met Jesus in the desert.
He was a lighted fractal on a page.
He was Woody Allen. And Shakespeare.
He was a girl named Rea.
I wonder what he or she will be
when I next see him or her?
It's all the same yet different
according to the Pop-Gnostics.

BANG
in the beginning
as in the ~~edn~~ end
(q. dramatic music)

Rea:

Yes, we left the next morning. Our nine days were up, and we had to get back to our regular lives. I could tell she was sad we were going. Even though she had only spent one night with us, I felt like she had become an honorary Edenite. Whatever *that's* supposed to mean (smiles).

She and I took a short hike after breakfast and she had a lot to say, like she was trying to squeeze in as much as she could before our time was up.

Like what?

Like, let me see. . . she told me about falling into the well, about her time in L.A., about the films she made, and. . . what? her angelwings? (smiles) Yea, she told me about those, too.

She not only told me she showed me her arm. I had never seen anything like it. It ran from about her elbow to her armpit and it was. . . I've never seen anything quite like it growing out of someone's arm or growing out of any body part, for that matter. . . it looked kind of like stubby metallic fins made out of steel mesh, or something. . . looked kind of cyberpunk (smiles).

She asked me if I thought it might be the start of a wing and I said I didn't know…to me it didn't look wing-like, but how can we judge phenomena we haven't seen before, right?

The very last thing?

We got back and she asked me if I knew The Cure, and did I like their music and I said I lovvved Robert Smith and she was super-excited and asked me if I could play any of their tunes on my sax, so I played Lovesong.

Play it now?

(Rea lifts her horn
and blows a stringent

slowburn opening
to Lovesong)

You know what she said to me after I finished? She said she
had named what I had done with music or what I sometimes did,
what she called this precise folding that she could feelsee, that's
how she put it, *feelsee,* and she called it 'Auralgami'. (laughs) Yes,
what with me being Japanese and all. I had never heard it put that
way before. Auralgami.

Yes, I was touched, yes

Piers's Journal, Undated

I want to go back
to where I came from
for real

Josef:

I must have been seven or eight when my grandfather first told me the story. I remember him saying to me—The Golem's name is Jossele, or Joseph, just like you. That made an impression on me. And the fact that the story was set in Prague, where we lived, that too made an impression. I remember thinking that this story hadn't taken place in some faraway land, it had happened right here, where I lived. The Golem and I, Jossele and Josef, had walked the same streets. When a story is close to home it holds special meaning for us.

Piers also felt a deep connection and resonance with the story, but she never said why. . . it was the one she wanted me to tell most often. . . and each time I told it, she listened with a most remarkable intensity, almost as if. . . how to say it. . . almost as if she were stalking the words (laughs).

Yes, I gave her the Golem puppet I had made. I wanted her to perform with it, but it was also meant as a special talisman. You see, I carved the Golem's eyes out of red onyx and onyx is known to be helpful in transforming negative emotions and releasing sorrow.

There are many versions of the legend, but the one my grandfather told me went like this: In the year 1580—and this, you understand, is a bit odd or unconventional, in that a specific year was usually not ascribed to a myth—anyway it was 1580, Prague, and an anti-Semitic priest was casting aspersions upon the Jewish people, accusing them of blood libel and other reprehensible acts. Blood libel, you see, meant that the Jews were alleged to be abducting and killing Christian babies and using their blood for religious ceremonies.

Rabbi Judah Loew ben Benzabel, an exalted teacher and mystic, knew that the persecution of his people would soon turn into widespread violence, and so he sought divine counsel through his dreams, and was instructed to use the Shem Hameforash, the true name of God, to create a golem. Rabbi Loew enlisted the aid of his son-in-law and a pupil, and together they were to represent three of the four needed elements—fire, water, and air—with the Golem representing the fourth, earth. After ritual purification the men read from Sefer Yeruzim, the Book of Creations, and then they went to the River Moldau, there Rabbi Loew sculpted a giant body out of river clay. Then Rabbi Loew's son-in-law walked seven times around the body, right to left, reading Zirufim, which are special Kabbalistic verses. The clay began to glow the color of fire. Then Rabbi Loew's pupil walked seven times around the body, left to right, and recited Zirufim. The fire-redness was displaced by water flowing through the body and the Golem grew hair and nails. Then Rabbi Loew completed the ritual by walking around the body once, and placed a slip of parchment, on which was written the true name of God, into the Golem's mouth.

Rabbi Loew bowed to the four directions and the three men recited—*And He breathed into his nostrils the breath of life and man became a living soul.*

You see, this was the manner in which God had given life to the nameless golem that became Adam.

In Psalm 139:16 from the Bible it reads:
Your eyes have seen my unformed golem
and in Your Book were all written the days
that were ordered for me

when as yet there were none of them

That's Adam, but in returning to our Golem, Jossele. . . my grandfather never gave specific details as to how he protected and saved the Jews, he just used to say—The Golem fulfilled the purpose for which he had been created.

And then the Golem went wrong. Or mad.

Again, no specific details from my grandfather, just a generalized climax—The protector became a monster and went on a rampage which Rabbi Loew put an end to by removing the true name of God.

You know, in a sense, the legend of the Golem introduced me to the world of gray. Before hearing that story, my world was very black and white—good and bad and right and wrong were sharply defined in my mind—but then after the Golem story, well things got a little murkier (smiles).

I can't say for certain, but I think my grandfather was intentionally vague at the end of the story, I think he left me blank spaces which would force me to participate in the story—morally, psychologically, imaginatively—and really consider the causal relationship between creation and destruction. . . I think he wanted *me* to think about it.

(Josef removes
a piece of yellow paper
folded foursquare
from his coat pocket

and unfolds it)

Since we're on this topic, here is something I thought you might find interesting. After I left the cave and returned to Prague, Piers and I exchanged letters in the mail. Our correspondence lasted about a year, and then a couple of my letters were returned: addressee unknown. From that point forward, I didn't receive any more letters from Piers. In one of the letters that had been returned to me, I had responded to a question Piers had posed about the nature of a golem, how I saw it *now*. . . I clearly remember that distinct quality of hers, the way in which she was always checking in to see if my thoughts or opinions or feelings about a subject or topic we had previously discussed had changed, and if so, how. . . it was marvelous, really, the manner in which she remained current through constant reappraisals and repeated inquiries, almost as if she wanted to exempt herself, and her relationship with others from becoming a dead or frozen thing.

I won't read you everything I wrote in the letter, but there's this one bit that I. . . well, let me just read it.

(Josef withdraws eyeglasses
from his shirtpocket
puts them on)

I think, the bottom line, Piers, is that one's protector is or can become one's destroyer. Angels are monsters in wait, same as monsters are angels awaiting transformative context. The two are one and to divide them is to breach the laws of wholeness, it is a violation of the Divine. Yet everywhere you will encounter people trying to destroy "golems" outside themselves, externalizing what is truly an internal matter, and assigning others the role of golem and naming them as such, even when the naming comes without words. How often do we judge, condemn, persecute and implicate without uttering a syllable?

The golem too is wordless, and yet it harbors the seeds of a secret vocabulary, the grammar of ruin and rebirth—*It* represents the process of becoming, and so I think the important question to ask: From who or what will its lighted directive come?

(Josef folds
the letter
places it back
in his coat pocket
removes the glasses
places them back
in his shirt pocket)

Is that the kind of stuff you're looking for?

Piers's Journal, July 23rd, 1985

I feel like a Jedi knight in training, like I'm Luke Skywalker to Josef's Obi Wan Kenobi. He's teaching me all kinds of techniques and lots about the history and tradition of shadow puppetry.

For example: I found it real interesting that in Java when they're performing what they call Wayang-Kulit, (which translates to "shadow-leather") the men sit behind the screen and get to see the actual puppets in action while the women sit in front of the screen and watch the projected shadows. Josef said when he was there he watched performances that would start at night and last all through the next day and that puppeteers, who were called dalangs, were highly respected artists.

And when it comes to the puppets of Chinese shadow theater, a red face means virtue and a black face means fidelity and a white face means treachery.

I am learning a lot and I was thinking how I only made Booboo and Jean to keep me company when I was laid up in bed and never thought about puppetry as an art form or as something I could do with my life, but after meeting Josef and seeing his devotion to craft… also this one thing he said that really stuck with me, he said shadow shows might be the closest we'll ever get to the truth about our souls. And his puppeteer friend calls them 'God's X-rays'.

Josef is showing me how much of it is in the wrist, and I've watched him with the slightest flick of his wrist turn a character into something truly pitiful and it is impossible to not feel their sorrow.

He also said everything begins and ends with controlling the center. He said you have to manage tension with a soft touch, that all true masters had a soft touch.

It's funny cuz Josef is very much a teacher but none of it feels like school. I am truly interested and want to listen to him. He speaks in a way that makes me feel gentle inside. Almost like he's taming me or something. Weird.

Piers's Journal, March 16th, 1985

Josef's cave is not very deep. More like a hollow. It's a bit of a bike ride to get here but I can bike ride a long ways, and I can do it in all kinds of weather. It's one of my special talents, I guess.

Josef lived in China for ten years, where he studied shadow puppetry with a couple of different masters, and he says that in China millions of people still live in caves, that they were functional habitats, not just in China, but all around the world.

Josef says he wound up in this cave because of a dream he had but he didn't tell me about the dream. I do know that before the cave he was living in Lemmon where he was taking care of a sick friend and after the sick friend died she came to him in a dream, the dream, and guided him to the cave. When Josef told me this he said it in a normal everyday kind of voice, which was strange cuz I don't know any grown men who talk like that: about dreams and dead friends and dead friends giving dream-advice. Then again, I don't know any grown men or grown women or grown anybody (or children) who live in caves.

What Josef has in the cave: lanterns, candles, blankets, sleeping bags, stacks of books, firewood, pots and pans and utensils, and steamer trunk filled with puppets. There are so many different kinds of puppets, most of them made by Josef. Some are painted and decorated, and others are just silhouettes. Then there's the weird ones like Clock-Man, who has a large clock face with three clock hands (frozen on noon, 2 and 6) and his body is made from connected bronze links, what looks like pirate earrings. And there's Florence with the curly hair and a melony bust and a hole where her stomach should be, and her legs are thin bamboo sticks wrapped in lace.

I like the Golem the most. He is gray and kind of looks like a robot-ghost and has these red eyes that haunt me. Josef says the next time I visit he'll tell me the story of the Golem.

I hope to get back to the cave this weekend. It's been easy keeping the cave a secret from Clark. Since Sylvia died, he's in another world. It's like Sylvia died and he became the ghost. Which is good, cuz he's not on top of me all the time and asking too many questions. I hope it stays that way.

Piers's Journal, April 20th, 1986

Today when I went to visit Josef he was crying. I had never seen him cry before. I'd also never seen a man cry before. Clark didn't cry at Sylvia's funeral and if he cried afterwards, I never saw it.

It was today that Josef found out about the U.S. bombing Libya (it happened on April 15) when he had gone to town for supplies and saw a newspaper. He has also heard two men in the store talking about Reagan and how it was nice to have someone in office that was more action than talk. Josef said when he got back to the cave the whole thing hit him hard.

He said he knew it was only a matter of time before America was in its next war. It was set up to happen that way. Then he told me something he had never told me before: that his son Jakob had died in a war. And lots of his friends had died in wars. After that he didn't say much else. He mostly sat quietly with his eyes closed, I think praying, and for a little while I watched him pray and then I left because I figured he wanted to be alone. After I left I felt bad for leaving. Should I have stayed with him? What could I have done? Maybe I should have prayed with him, I don't know. I did pray for Sylvia because I didn't want her to suffer so much, but she did suffer a lot, especially at the end, and why is it that good people suffer? Or maybe it's because she was good that she suffered, she was too good and was stepped on by others and if you're stepped on too many times over a long period you wind up with cancer because you didn't speak up or fight back or let yourself be heard.

And the meek shall inherit the earth. Yea right. More like the meek shall inherit the early grave.

Piers's Journal, March 16th, 1986

It's all turning to shit.

Clark found out about the cave and about Josef and he was furious and told me not to go back there anymore and that if I did there'd be big consequences. He also said he was gonna get me help, that I needed help for a while now and I actually laughed right in his face and I thought for sure he was gonna hit me, but he didn't and how could I not laugh when he's saying I'm the one who needs help? The mirrors in this house are blacked out. It's a wonder he can shave without cutting his throat.

I'm not gonna let him stop me from doing what I need to do. The cave has meant everything to me. It's been my sanctuary and my school and Josef has taught me so much, has given me so much, and how could I possibly explain something like that to Clark, Mr. Hammer and Nails and I pledge allegiance to the bones, Mr. Middle Amerikkka—we are aliens to each other and that's how I want it to stay.

Belle Fourche Gazette, April 9th, 1986
Cave Man Questioned
by Charles Kubel

In an incident that occurred this past Tuesday at Safeway, Clark Lund, owner of Lund's Hardware, confronted Josef Sarka, the town's "old man in the cave."

Both men were shopping when Lund reportedly approached Sarka and began shouting at him while jabbing his finger into the old man's chest. Officer Klasko, who happened to be in the store, separated the two men, with Lund shouting, "That man's a pervert and he'd better keep away from my daughter!"

While specific details are not known, it seems that Lund's thirteen-year-old adopted daughter, Pierangela, had been spending time with Sarka in his cave, with Lund alleging that their relationship was "inappropriate and indecent."

Sarka, a native of Czechoslovakia, has lived in a small cave at the edge of town, near the Redwater River, for nearly three years. While regarded by many as an eccentric and a loner, Sarka's behavior and action have never warranted concern… until now.

Belle Fourche police plan to investigate Lund's allegations.

Sarka declined comment for this story.

She had risen, and now at last a fear assailed him.

"What is it?" he cried, shrinking.

"I will turn up the light," she said, "and then you can see for yourself."

For about the only time in his life that I know of, Peter was afraid.

"Don't turn up the light," he cried.

—J.M. Barrie, *Peter Pan*

All that she had kept at a distance began closing in on her.
The ending meant returning to herself in slow motion,
a pace that would not only force her to bear witness but to do
so in reverse.
A backlog of secret touches that had turned her inside-out,
and even though she had walked around that way, inside-out,
no one had ever noticed.

Piers's Journal, September 1st, 1984

I got the idea from a story I saw on the news a couple of nights ago. The story was about a boy from Omaha who wrote his name and phone number on a balloon then released the balloon into the sky, and five days later it landed in Singapaw, where it was found by a fisherman.

I am amazed that a balloon can travel that far. How many other balloons have made it that far, I wonder. Those balloons were not reported on the news, so we'll never know. But I bet there's a lot.

I have decided to try my own experiment. Today I went to the store and bought three helium balloons. On each one I wrote something different.

Pierangela Lund of Belle Fourche Needs Your Help
Can Somebody Put an End to This, Your Friend, Pierangela Lund
Please Help, Your Friend, Pierangela Lund

Tomorrow when my uncle is at work I am going to set the balloons free.
I wonder what will happen?

One of Piers's balloons,
which it made as far as the Black Hills (77 miles),
before meeting its fate in a wrathful mob
of storm clouds

Please

A white room,
like burnished ivory,
like karmic burden.

Close-up on the back of a head and neck.
The head is shaved,
its scant fuzz like graphite shading.
The neck is a pale shoot, a fawn's neck.
The head and neck loom in the foreground of the frame.
In the background, at a medium distance, is a body, visible only
from the chest down.
Shirtless, taut, cubed stomach, cocoa-skinned, bladed hips
sinking
into skinnylegs cased in tight-tight electric blue leatherpants.
The body shuttles back and forth back and forth,
an interrogator on a horizontal pulley.
The white wall in the background is fringed in a lacy black
curtain.
The shot is soft-focus, visually matching the interrogator's
valium-inflected monotone.

Body: Did you do it a lot?
Head: *We* didn't do it. He did it. He.
Body: So it was done *to* you?
Head: Yes.
Body (addressing someone off-screen) Make note of that.
How did it begin?
Head: I don't remember.

Body: When did it happen?

Head: You mean time of day and stuff?

Body: Yes.

Head: I don't remember.

(There is a brief silence. We notice that the lacy curtain stirs, as if fingered by wind, indicating that there is a source of ventilation in the room.)

Body: But it happened, didn't it?

Head: Yea, (pause) I can tell you how it ended.

Body: Go ahead. If you'd like.

Head: Right after I turned twelve he asked me if I wanted it to stop. He said I was getting older and it was probably a good idea if we stopped. If I wanted to. That was exactly how he put it.

Body: And what did you say?

Head: I said okay, though I didn't really know what I was saying okay to.

Body: What do you mean?

Head: I wasn't sure what we were talking about.

Body: You didn't know?

Head: When I thought about what he said, I felt like I was sticking my head in a black hole.

Body: So you didn't know?

Head: I don't fucking know what I knew, I told you that I felt like my head was in a black hole, isn't that enough?

Body (to the off-screen person): Please make note of the black hole.

(pause) The photo that you gave us . . . is that him?

Head: No. It's someone who looks like him.

Body: What do you mean *someone who looks like him*?

Head: I mean one day I saw a man on the street who looked like him and I snapped a photo because I thought that one day, maybe, I don't know, maybe one day it would be useful.

Body: The photo?

Head: The photo, yes.

Body: Useful as in. . . evidence?

Head: Yea, maybe.

Body: You do understand that the evidence is inadmissible?

Head: Inadmissible?

Body: We can't use it. It's not the same man. It's someone who, in your own words, is *someone who looks like him*.

(Silence. The Head moves ever so slightly, what could be construed as a spasm psychic or emotional in nature).

Body: When he said to you, *we can stop if you'd like*, how did that make you feel?

Head: I didn't know what he was talking about.

Body: Pretend that you did.

(Silence)

Body: I said—

Head: I was fucking pissed, okay? That he said we could stop. *We.*

Body: Because you weren't part of it.

Head: Because I wasn't part of it, right.

Body: Because you were somewhere else?

Head: I was somewhere else, yes.

Body (to the off-screen person) Please make note of that. She was somewhere else.

Head: But what I said to him was—Okay.

Body: Okay, meaning you didn't want it to continue?

Head: Yes.

Body: And so it stopped?

Head: It stopped. Yes. It had been in my life and then it wasn't in my life. Like it had never happened at all.

Body: How did that make you feel?

(Silence)

Body (to off-screen person): Make note of her silence at. . . 6:47 into the tape.

Head: Please do not make note of my silence.

Body: But you didn't say anything?

Head: Fuck you. There, I said something.

Piers's Journal, Undated

I was born a beautiful boy with wings. ~~This much I know.~~

~~Whether or not others saw my boy or my wings, I don't know. But I could feel them. My boy, my wings. They were a part of me as much as my soul (which others cannot see).~~

~~They still are a part of me, even though the wings have gone. They fell apart, feather by feather, and then were gone. It was like having an angel on your back at all times, watching over you, giving comfort, and then the angel disappears. The absence of that angel kills you inside. Kills certain parts of you.~~

~~There is the memory of that angel, of those wings, and sometimes that makes it worse but mostly it makes it better because I am inspired to grow new wings. I have been trying. I have read about people growing wings. I have done my research. It is not impossible. It is categorized under impossible but there a lot of things categorized impossible which really are possible.~~

I intend to grow my wings back.

~~As for the beautiful boy that I am, he's still there inside me. He powers my actions and movements and choices. Well some of my choices. Some of my choices, if I'm not mistaken, are powered by demons. Or ghosts. Or both. They smother the boy, like haunted shawls or something. Then the boy can't breathe or move and the demon or ghost takes over. It is, I guess, a sort of possession.~~

~~I see that beautiful boy inside me and feel him and want to send him home. But he can't go, not until he has wings again. Not~~

~~until I have wings. When we have our wings things will be different.~~

~~Sometimes the memory of the wings and the boy fades, no that's not it … sometimes the feeling behind the memory of the wings and the boy fades and I need to remind myself again and again and again~~

I am a beautiful boy with wings
I am a beautiful boy with wings
I am a beautiful boy with wings

I may have written this line more than any other line in my journals.

It is my beloved echo.

Piers's Journal, Undated

Yellow is the color of my sad. My true sad. I used to think it was blue but now I know it's yellow.

Yellow is an emergency siren. Some will tell you it's red, but they are wrong. The pause is much more emergency siren than the stop.

I think the time I spent in the cave with Josef helped me to realize this. The coming and going between dark and light, the secrecy and the exposure.

Back then I couldn't name it, but now I have a list. Not names, but the right words, placeholders for feeling, a sense of order.

1. Yellow blinds you with hurt, a soft blinding hurt. Fuzzy. Like getting drunk on too much sun.
2. Yellow is a low droning in your head. A graveyard of bees.
3. The bees cast shadows. That is what you are seeing. You hear their buzzing, but you see their shadows. That is the way Memory works.
4. When I was at the bottom of the well looking up, yellow was a promise. It was a faraway-seeming promise that demanded I grow taller or fly or do something impossible.
5. The tears of grief are yellow. My hands have held them.
6. Yellow is the glowing badge of disease, the survivor's worry.
7. I have looked into Van Gogh's yellows. They are omens and signals. They are ravens masquerading as sunlight.
8. Yellow is deadly to a Nocturne, the soft killer, the slippered rapist, the silent assassin. It gets inside you and scrambles the system, wreaks havoc, but subtly so.
9. Yellow is the softest of last kisses, the saddest of moons.

10. Yellow eats away the necessary dark inside you. Like acid lemonade.

11. The girl in the yellow raincoat is dead. Or never existed. I made her up because I needed something to chase, a reason.

12. Though I did see a girl in a yellow raincoat in a photo. She was standing next to my mother. My mother was holding an umbrella over both their heads and the girl was wearing a yellow raincoat and everything went well together: mother, daughter, umbrella, raincoat. It made sense.

13. Yellow is the canary that was swallowed by the dog. The canary sings inside the dog's dark.

14. There never was a girl in a yellow raincoat. I made her up. Just because.

Max:

I'm not really sure what happened to him. The whole thing boggles me.

He's been at this thing a lot longer than I have and I was taking my cues from him and. . . he seemed pretty together, pretty professional ya know?

Me, I know I'm professional, but that's *me*. I know what to expect from myself, but other people. . . when it comes down to it you don't really know what's going on inside other people's heads.

That morning I went to his room and knocked and there was no answer. I figured okay, he probably got up early and went for a walk or something. I didn't give it much thought. I went to the coffeeshop, came back, knocked, no answer, tried again in an hour, nothing. So then I checked in with the guy at the front to see if he knew anything and he told me yea, your friend checked out early this morning and he left this envelope for you. Inside the envelope was a note which read

I couldn't go on in the same way
Good luck being Max

So there's those two lines and beneath them there's a passage, hold on let me get the note

(retrieves the note from his pocket)

Kiliminjaro is a snow-covered mountain, 19,710 feet high, and is said to be the highest mountain in Africa. Its Western summit is called the Masai "Ngaje Ngai"—

I have no idea if I pronounced that right

—the Home of God. Close to the summit there is a dried and

frozen carcass of a leopard. No one has explained what the leopard was seeking at that altitude.

Sincerely, Ernest Hemingway

That's what it says. I have no idea what the hell he was getting at I'm not in the guy's head but—me? Not really. I read The Killers to prepare for our job and in high school I remember reading, what's the name of that one, it was the one where the father's a jockey and he gets killed when a horse falls on top of him and his son sees it. . . "My Old Man", yea that's it.

Yea I told DeLeon and he didn't say much. Just told me to forget the job and come back to L.A. I told him I could do the job by myself, but he said no, come back to L.A. So that's what I did.

We see a medium distance shot of the back of Piers's head.

Then, starting in the foreground, at an angle, a gun floats into the frame.

A revolver. We cannot tell if it is a real gun or a toy one.

The gun hovers, silhouetted fingers wrapped around its handle, then it glides toward the back of Piers's head, a piranha with intent.

When its snub-nose makes contact with Piers's head, middle of the back, it presses in and the screen goes black.

The screen stays black

We are left in suspense.

Malingering suspense.

3-4-5-6-7. . .

And then: the whiny death-cry of sirens, the slashing red lights.

We hear the sirens, we see the flashing, and then the screen goes black again.

Several beats.

Return to the noisy bright sirens, what amounts to garlands of noise being stuffed into our ears and eyes.

Silence.

It goes on like this for a while, perhaps for the duration of an ambulance ride.

Black soft silence, noisy bright sirens.

Cut to a long shot of a young Piers,

running and running through a green field dotted with white flowers.

Running and running, matchstick arms akimbo, dressed in a blue and white checked summer dress.

There is a sudden, slow, piercing recognition; it is as if the camera, the scene, has transfused feeling into us.

We feel the sun beating like soft fleshy miniature wings inside us, a tease, a flicker, a feathery brush. It is the gilded feel that everything is alright, and everything will always be alright.

And then come the crows, like handlebar moustaches, like cursive blights.

They are raining down out of the sky, and they rain and they rain, and the scene no longer feels summer-good, that sense of everything is alright and will always be alright is blackened by omen.

The bad is coming. Treason. The bad and Treason and there's nothing we can do to stop it.

It is now as if the camera, the scene, has transfused powerlessness into us.

We can rage and curse. We can remind ourselves that we are audience, and there is distance.

There is much we can do, we have options.

Yet none of that changes the fact that we are powerless to stop what is coming.

It seems like a lifetime ago
that I was huffing Sike
and hanging out in the Attic
and now I'm at the beginning of time
where there is no water
I miss the Pacific
and no palm trees
and no traffic
and no streets
just lots of lonely
eating me
and I miss huffing Sike
and how did Trink put it
more Childhood than Childhood
the appleness of apples, grace
I miss that
now I've got fucking blades growing out of my arm
and I'm gonna die facedown
in billion yr old fossils and clinkers
shit

To grow wings is not so simple
but the human starts off with
astralwings anyway
realwings require shapeshifting
and. . ..
—fragment from untitled manifesto,
author unknown

Just keep walking
and looking at things
look at the moon looking at you
is it watching over you
in a good wayin a not so good way
is it indifferent
ask the moon sincerely
Are you my mother
keep walking and talking
and looking at things

Belle Fourche Gazette, July 29th, 1979—
Pierangela Lund,
the six-year-old
who fell into the well
this past Tuesday
seems to be recovering nicely…
"She's watching a lot of TV
and indulging her sweet tooth,"

My mother bathed in yellow
too much yellow
it hurt

At present:
Henry gravely considering
his lungs
and worrying about Jacques
who it seems
by the way he's repeatedly
licking his forepaws
is worrying about Henry

At present:
Trink thoroughly strung out
on heroin
his new drug of choice

Row row row yr boat
gently down the stream
if you see a crocodile
don't forget to scream
and it would've been nice if I had
Booboo & Jean here to sing with me
why did I bury them
I want them back
and now they're lost forever

because you're so stupid
so impulsive and now
the very first friends
you had are gone
the very first
not a very good friend
are you
not a very good parent
or caretaker or whatever
you bury your friends
your children
on a whim
and then you cry about it
but you don't even cry
you bitch & moan
o poor me
my friends are gone
row row row yr boat
sadly down the stream
now you row it all alone
cuz yer so fucking stupid
and careless and…

"compulsively addicted
to shadows, and to high contrasts
between light and dark,
the noir screen offers
a cornucopia of patterns of chiaroscuro,
as pools of shadow surround
and sometimes overtake

small centers of light"
—*Film Noir: The Dark Side of the Screen,* Foster Hirsch

"The nightmarishly disorted décor
of German Expressionist films
and their certain stimmung ('mood')
through shifting chiaroscuro lighting
were expressions of the distorted mental
and emotional states they sought to portray"
—*A History of Narrative Film,* David A. Cook

I remember Josef saying
There is good silence golden silence
but there is also silence that is
malignant and soul-killing
silence that destroys people
from the inside-in

the existential spinning of gears
like clockwork
like tears
—Simone Lefleur

On October 13th, 1989
Woody Allen released
Crimes and Misdemeanors
and on Christmas Day 1990
he will release *Alice*
inspired by Fellini's

257

Just keep walking
one step after the next
after the next
left right left
right left right
like keeping pace to a metronome
or broken watch
just keep walking
and looking at things

1
2
3
4
5
6
7
8
9

"Oh, how glad I am"
whispered Okiku's ghost
after she was freed by
a holy man who spoke the magic word
which was a number

10

Remember remember:
He a young grungestyle Abe Lincoln
She a rabbiteared saxophonist
Remember remember

. . . .

Henry's dad so handsome
and I realize that
I've never seen beneath
Henry's eyepatch
what's there

. . . .

The Bureau of Laundred Undergarments
that's funny
and what about The Dresser for Unwashed Panties
that's funny too
laugh Piers laugh

. . . .

I've touched myself downthere
so many times since
how many days has it been
I think I'm developing stigmata
or my poor pussy is

. . . .

Rea's long hipless waist
Autumn's lush black hair
Anya's glacial face
a tense & jittery
fittingtogether of parts

259

she & her
she & her
she & her
such unnatural need

You
Soft and only
You
Lost and lonely
You
Strange as angels
Dancing on the deepest oceans
Twisting in the water
You're just like a dream—
The Cure, "Just Like Heaven"

and you may be
a beautiful boy with wings
Piers
but what the fuck
is this inhuman shit
growing out of your arm
this is not a wing to be
noway
and I worry that my arm
will have to be cut off
and how I wish I could place

my worries like worry stones
inside a sax like Rea
and blow em out into fairy dust
wouldn't that be nice
wouldn't that be something

At present:
Rea gigging at Bruno's
in the Mission
blowing *Over the Rainbow*
with felicity & ease

At present:
Autumn watching *Growing Pains*
in the livingroom with her sister
and cousin and brother
and father

At present:
Anya finally tackling
three days worth
of dirty dishes
in the sink

The 1964 version of *The Killers*
was Ronald Reagan's last film
before entering politics
and the only film in which he played
a villain

At present:
Joe is reading
Hemingway's *The Sun Also Rises*
and had been marking passages, i.e.,
"I did not care what it was all about.
All I wanted to know was how to live in it.
Maybe if you found out how to live in it
you learned from that what it was all about."

Just keep walking
and talking
and noticing
and naming things

At present:
Josef is strolling across
the Charles Bridge and
thinking about his dead son Jakob

The *Golem* (1915)	*The Golem* *and the* *Dancing Girl* (1917)	The Golem: How He Came Into the World (1920)

The Golem trilogy of films, each one co-directed by and starring Paul Wegener, were part of the German Expressionist period of cinema. The first two are considered "lost films", with only fragments surviving, while the third one, a full film, ranks alongside *The Cabinet of Dr. Caligari* as a classic in silent German horror.

Audio-clip, May 1988
(correlating to the film *Cabinet*)

Int: When you were younger
what did you want to be?
Piers: Dead
or transcendent.
Int: As a kid
did you have a favorite hiding place?
Piers: My Aunt's closet.
Her dresses smelled like rose perfume.
Int: Name your best memory from childhood?
Piers (pause) Playing with Booboo & Jean.
The first time I played with Booboo & Jean.
Int: What is your first conscious memory?
Piers: I don't know.
Int.: Tell us a story
that best exemplifies the spirit of your childhood.
Piers: (tells the story of chasing the white fox,
falling into the well, the aftermath)

At present:
Uncle Clark in his woodshop
splitting a board
on a bandsaw

At present:
Aunt Sylvia's voice
somewhere in the dark
crying *Mea culpa*

At present:
DeLeon is picking up
his daughter Zoe from
acting class where he will be
informed by Zoe's drama teacher
Ms. Vasquez that
*Zoe has an incredible gift
for mimicry and improv*

At present:
Max #1
and Max #2
who have never met
(and never will)
happen to be eating at the same
Jack in the Box on Sunset

At present:
Henry is wondering why he never
got married never had a kid
never saw the ocean
never did this or that
a Neverland of nots
and didnts
binding Henry

Wonder
what do I wonder now
I wonder about you Trink
where you are
and how scared you must have been
when the Trenchcoats took you away
and me and you really are wreckmates
cuz the same two Trenchcoats are after me
well can't say for sure it's the same two
but me and you are a coupla fuckup wreckmates
that I can say for sure

Body: The photo?
Head: The photo, yes.
Body: Useful as in. . . evidence?
Head: Yea, maybe.
Body: You do understand
that the evidence is inadmissible?
Head: Inadmissible?
Body: We can't use it. It's not the same man.
It's someone who, in your own words, is
someone who looks like him.

Notes on Lighting:
If you leave a print or photograph
out in the light too long
the image will eventually disappear.
Light, in this respect,
is a double-edged sword.
Exposure,
and the fade of exposure,
in equal measures.
Light is also a traitor,
an enigma, a crisis,
and an outlet for grief.

palsied, unlit, unfeeling,
an embryo pickled
in a false womb

266

At present:
the Golem
is lying inert in the attic
of the Old New Synagogue
in Josefov, Prague

At present:
Henry is eating Chinese
and watching reruns of
All Through the Years

At present:
Gwen is soaking away
the residue of a double-shift
in a hot bath

Just keep walking
and talking
and looking
and naming

Publicity still
of Doris Day as Calamity Jane
in the 1953 musical comedy *Calamity Jane*
(Cowboyhat
 a battered dusty saucer
covering her tiltedright head
mouth maniacally agape
emitting laughter or riotous whoop
cloudchalked widesky
behind her
doublebarrel shotgun
leveled in two hands
pointed at someone
we cannot see)

"It is a good thing
that you don't know
how your mother has to live
out here these hectic days.
I mind my own business
but always remember that is
one thing the world hates
is a woman who minds her
own business. They are telling
awful things about meNone of it
is trueevery man I speak to
I'm accused of being an immoral slut.
My dear—someday you may come out here
in this west and will hear a lot of
lies about your mother. . .
I suppose now that I am joining
Buffalo Bill's Wild West show
they will know for sure down deep
in their hypocritical hearts that I am
bound for hell."
—Calamity Jane to her daughter, 1893

"Four years have slipped by
and I am back in Deadwood.
I am tired and feel so old.
I am nursing again.
I can always fall back on that.
I got so lonely for our old west
and so disgusted with gadding all over the world."

—Calamity Jane to her daughter, July 1898

*"Winter is here again and I am down here on
the Clark Forks for awhile. This life is a long
hideous nightmare. This country is beautiful
but I am growing to hate it, because it has taken
from me everything I have ever loved.
It took Bill from me, it was the cause of having
to give you up. It has wrecked me, this country.
I am not old, Janey, but I feel as though I had
reached the end of my rope."*
—Calamity Jane to her daughter, 1898

are you my mother
are you my mother
are you my mother

On May 15th, 1990
"The Portrait of Dr. Gachet"
by Vincent Van Gogh
will fetch a record 82.5 million
at a New York art auction.
Note the rumpled, melancholic expression
etched into Dr. Gachet's face,
note the plasmic longing.

Body: When he said to you
we can stop if you'd like
how did that make you feel?
Head: I didn't know what he was talking about.
Body: Pretend that you did.
(Silence)
Body: Make note of her silence at. . .
6:47 into the tape.
Head: Please do not make note of my silence.
Body: But you didn't say anything?

"Dear Janey—I guess my diary is just about fin-
ished. I am going blind but I can still see to write this
yet but I can't keep on to live an avaricious
old age. All hope is dead forever, Janey, What
have I ever done except to make one blunder
after another? All I have left are these
little pictures of you and your father. I can't go on
blind and the doctor told me yesterday
that in 2 months I would be absolutely blind. Oh how
I wish I had my life to live over."
Two months later
I'm sick and haven't long to live. I am taking
many secrets with me, Janey. What I am
and what I might have been. I'm not as black as I
am paintedI want you to believe that My eyes
have cheated me out of the pleasure I could get
from looking at your photos. . .

Fuck you
there
I said something

Henry:

I went to the gate on the sixth day to meet her, like we planned, but she wasn't there. So I waited and waited and she didn't come, so I went looking for her or her tent and I searched for hours but I couldn't find her, not a trace.

I was freaked out and felt responsible because hiding out in the badlands had been my idea, and the next morning I took off from work and spent the whole day looking for her. I asked some people I bumped into if they had seen her, they hadn't, and then I ran into a guy walking his horse who said he had seen her about a half-hour earlier. He pointed out where and then decided to walk with me to show me, the guy's name was Jose and he lived just outside the badlands and went there regularly to walk his horse...

When we found her, she was huddled in her overcoat, sitting on a rock, just staring out. I went to her and saw that her face was pretty badly windburned and sunburned and even though I was standing right next to her, she didn't react to my presence, she didn't see me, and I was worried that something had happened to her eyes and then I was worried that something had happened to her mind because she seemed not there, but when I spoke her name, she responded right away, Henry, she said in this hoarse whisper, but she still didn't look at me. It was weird, like she could hear me but not see me, like my voice was there, but I wasn't.

When I asked her if she could stand up and walk she said she was dizzy and weak and nauseous and I knew she was dehydrated and gave her water to drink. When she took the water from me and drank from the bottle, it was then that I became real to her, or more than just a voice. Jose, god bless his soul, suggested that we get her onto Lucy, Lucy was his horse, and she would carry her back. So we did that, and when she was on Lucy she just kind of slumped forward and Jose told her to hold on to Lucy's neck and that Lucy would take care of her she was a special horse.

I carried her backpack and sacrificed the tent and gear since she had no idea where she left everything. We walked back to the gate where I had parked the truck and Jose told me to follow him back to his house, which was only fifteen minutes away, and we could tend to her health.

Decisions had to be made.

The first was Gwen's decision to invite Piers to stay with her, offering what had once been her son's bedroom.

Piers thanked her and said she'd think about it and the next day told Gwen she was leaning toward leaving Redline.

This forced Gwen to make another decision, one that perhaps was not hers to make, and after a spell of conscientious deliberation, she informed Piers that Henry had been diagnosed with Stage IV Lung Cancer.

Piers was a little bewildered, a little stunned.

When did he find out?

About two weeks ago.

Piers recalled how no one had told her Aunt Sylvia was sick until she was hospitalized. And then she died three weeks later.

Though Piers had known something was wrong with her aunt, she hadn't known exactly what it was, nor did she know its tragic implications. Her aunt would refer to the unspecified shadow that hung over her health in cryptic and cursory terms: *I'm not feeling myself today. . . my health is giving me a little trouble. . . My body's having a rough time of it.*

So Henry's prognosis is not good?

No, Gwen confirmed. The cancer's infected both lungs and has spread to other parts of his body.

Piers took a reflective pause, then—So you think I should stay?

No, I don't think that at all, I think you should do what you wanna do. . . I just thought you should know because, well because it seems like you and Henry have become pretty good friends.

Pretty good friends? Her and Henry? The notion, once it sunk in, struck Piers as slightly amusing and ridiculous. And true.

Now it was Piers's turn to make a decision. Should she stay in Redline? If she decided to leave, where would she go? Should she risk L.A.? If only she knew where Trink was. There was always Josef and Prague, but that seemed to be a bit of a stretch at the moment.

If she stayed in Redline, for how long? This town wasn't meant for her, she wanted something else, somewhere else.

That night, lying in bed, Piers fantasized about all the places she could go and what those places would be like. She had the freedom to choose and if she didn't like the place she had chosen, she could choose another place, and this run of possible choices inspired a sense of giddy spaciousness which ballooned within her. The next morning, before Gwen left for work, Piers told her— I'm going to stay.

Okay, Gwen smiled and nodded.

I don't know for how long, but for now.

Okay, Gwen repeated.

That afternoon, when Henry went into Red's for lunch, Gwen told him that she had told Piers about his condition and that she was really-really sorry, but Piers was talking about leaving town and she probably should have checked with him before saying anything, and she hoped he could forgive her.

Henry said he wasn't mad and there was nothing to forgive.

You sure, Gwen double-checked.

I'm sure, Henry smiled, and considered placing his hand over Gwen's hand which was laid on the counter, but feared misinterpretation of intent. Or correct interpretation of deepdown intent.

Henry had decisions to make, too. About chemo and about surgery. About Jacques.

After a third cup of coffee Henry worked up the nerve to ask Gwen if she would consider taking Jacques in if, as Henry put it, I punch the clock before he does.

Gwen said she would.

Henry felt relieved and crossed Jacque's future housing situation off his list of worries.

Piers hadn't left the house in five days, except to hang out on the porch or in the backyard, where she'd lounge on a beach chair and bask in the sun.

While she couldn't recall exactly what had happened to her in the badlands, (the whole thing felt like a distant memory coiled in gauze) she understood that she had experienced a sort of crack-up, a psychic upheaval, and that parts of herself had gone away, had flown off in fragments in different directions, and within the safe harbor that was Gwen's home, some parts had returned or were returning. Other parts, she imagined, the ones that had traveled greater distances, might take longer to return, or were perhaps gone forever.

Piers's restorative regimen comprised of sunbathing, writing in her journal, listening to music (Bowie's *changesbowie* and The Smith's *Louder than Bombs* receiving the most airplay), taking several extended showers throughout the day, and watching daytime TV. She had never before watched soap-operas and gameshows and it felt like she was gorging on audio-visual jellybeans or marshmallows.

One afternoon, Piers, motivated by boredom, thought it would be fun to rummage through Gwen's stuff. She entered Gwen's bedroom for the first time and there it was, hanging from a wooden peg protruding from the closet door. A bright yellow raincoat.

Piers felt a catch in her throat and her breathing accelerated.

At first, she just stared at the raincoat, as if appraising an exotic specimen, and then she went over to it and ran her fingers along the length of its arm. Her touch registered peach fuzz.

She took the raincoat down from the peg and tried it on, looping its belt to cinch the waist.

She looked at herself in the vanity mirror mounted on the bureau.

The mirror showed her a waif with pixie-length chestnut hair, playing dress-up in a yellow raincoat that fit big.

Piers struck different modeling poses and imagined that someone behind the mirror, or inside of it, was taking pictures of her, a fashion photographer urging her on—That's perfect, baby, now give me that look, you know the one, great, great, now the lips, more, more, set them to babe-pout. Excellent, and now the eyes, bigger, bigger, put a spell on me, great, great, now spin around, spin like you haven't got a care in the world, you're worry-free. Yep, there you go, beautiful, keep spinning, keep spinning, now hold it.

Piers spent the next fifteen minutes engaged in her imaginary photo shoot and then took off the raincoat and hung it back on the peg.

She stared at the raincoat, considered its forlorn creases and folds.

I need it, came the resolute directive in Piers's mind.

Her first instinct was to steal it, but that instinct was met by resistance—You can't steal from Gwen. She has taken you into her home and treated you kindly and a line's got to be drawn somewhere.

And so Piers, running counter to her impulse, decided that she would ask Gwen if she could have the raincoat or if she would sell it to her.

One last covetous look at the raincoat, and then Piers closed the bedroom door and went out into the backyard to sunbathe.

Piers's Journal, May 10th, 1990

The sun is strong today. It has been strong and honey and golden pretty much every day. Post-badlands, this is part of what I need: sufficient doses of warmth and sunlight to nourish me.

I haven't seen or heard from Henry since I found out he has cancer. Is he avoiding me? Am I avoiding him? Well, I guess I'm pretty much avoiding everyone and everything outside the house right now. Any reality beyond the porch and the backyard seems to be off-limits.

I wonder if the Trench-coats are still in town? Henry, after having rescued me from the badlands (imagine that, I was rescued like some dumbass lost in the desert, non-princess,) told me he hadn't seen the Trench-coats around town. How long ago was that, two weeks, maybe three?

So either they're gone or they're hiding out in the shadows waiting to make their move, and I hate not-knowing and I also hate the fact, I <u>fucking hate it,</u> that I am scared and I blame part of that on the badlands, whatever it did to me, whatever shit it stirred up, and part of it is just commonsense. Two men who are real and not fictitious boogeymen are after you, Piers, and they wanna kill you or maim you, so you have every right to be scared. Still, I fucking hate it.

Anyway, I'll need to leave the house, and soon. Gwen laid it out for me the first night: she said I could stay as long as I wanted, but I had to get a job and contribute. It's the first time in my life anyone ever told me I had to get a job. She didn't say it mean or bossy, just matter of fact. She knows I'm going through something right now, that I'm licking psychic wounds, or whatever, so she hasn't badgered me, but I also know that woundlicking has a statute of limitations like everything else, so yea, a fucking job.

Why am I even staying in Redline?

Even if the Trench-coats have gone they might come back and Trink used to say if you keep moving the demons have a harder time tracking you down and here I am staying put like a sitting fucking duck. Stupid.

I haven't touched my puppets or even done hand-shadows since I've been at Gwen's. Not feeling it right now, and I think it has something to do with the loss of Booboo and Jean. I vaguely remember having done something to them. Your oldest childhood friends are gone, Piers, and it's your fault. What did I do to them? I still have the Golem, but he's not Booboo and Jean.

Maybe I should write a letter to Josef? It's been awhile, I miss him, and maybe he'll invite me to stay with him in Prague, maybe he'll even spring for the plane ticket. I heard that the Czech girls are stunning and how cool would it be to have a romantic affair with a Czech siren far, far away from everything I've ever known?

I don't know
where I'm going
from here
but I promise
it won't be boring
—David Robert Jones, a.k.a., David Bowie, a.k.a., Ziggy Stardust, a.k.a., the Thin White Duke, a.k.a., etc, etc.

Spring, after one final dust-swirling siege of high winds, gave way to summer.

Piers's life had acquired varying degrees of stability, an almost benign normalcy.

Gwen had gotten her a job as a dishwasher at Red's. It was either busser or dishwasher, and Piers opted for the latter, where social interaction would be limited and she could listen to her Walkman while performing her duties. She worked at Red's three to four days a week and on weekend afternoons performed puppet shows in the plaza, which, as promised by the mayor, had been showing steady signs of growth and vitality. A half-dozen new stores had opened, a farmer's market had been installed on Saturdays and there was talk of a wealthy Texan opening up a movie theater in the condemned Toreador Hotel.

One of the stores that had recently opened was Lucy's Book Bin, a used book store and book exchange. Lucy, a septuagenarian bibliophile, had amassed a staggering and diverse collection of books over her lifetime and decided it was time to share her treasury with the public.

Every inch of her tiny store was monopolized by bookcases and bookshelves, creating the narrowest of aisles in which to browse. It was there, amidst faded, worn and weathered texts, and Lucy, seated behind the counter, chain-smoking Camels, spectacles precariously perched on her long, veiny nose, that Piers discovered and fell head-over-heels in love with Anne Sexton and her poetry.

She had been scouring a bookshelf when her curiosity was piqued by a dog-eared paperback titled *Live or Die*. She took the book down from the shelf, opened it, and the first thing she read was the Author's Note:

To begin with, I have placed these poems (1962-1966) in the order in which they were written with all due apologies for the fact that they read like a fever chart for a bad case of melancholy. But I thought the order of their creation might be of interest to some readers, and, as André Gide wrote in his journal, "Despite every resolution of optimism, melancholy occasionally wins out: man has decidedly botched up the planet."

Pier proceeded to sit on a footstool near a window and devoured the poems in a single sitting.

It felt as if this Anne Sexton had passed lightning into her, and she continued sitting there, woozy, charred, and relishing the aftershocks.

When she brought the book to the counter to buy it, Lucy held it at a distance from her face, squinted, and pursed her lips approvingly—Ah yes, Anne Sexton.

Piers confessed that she had never heard of her before, and, as if on cue, Lucy launched into a spirited exposition on Sexton's troubled life and eventual suicide, and her impact on modern poetry. Lucy said that Sexton had meant a lot to her as a young woman, especially a young woman growing up Catholic in the 1950s, and she was glad young women were still discovering and appreciating Sexton.

Lucy had four more Sexton books of poetry in stock—*All the Pretty Ones, Transformations, Love Poems,* and *The Awful Rowing Toward God*—as well as *Anne Sexton: A Self-Portrait in Letters.* Piers bought them all for a grand total of $5 and devoted the rest of her day to her newest crush.

Piers's Journal, July 3rd, 1990

~~I want to eat~~
~~Anne Sexton for breakfast~~
~~want to swallow her whole~~
~~like flammable air and breathe fire~~
~~burning down all the~~

I want to eat Anne Sexton for breakfast
want to swallow her whole
~~like flammable air and breath fire~~

I want to eat
Anne Sexton for breakfast
like toxic cereal
like bacon fat
~~like egg yolks swallowed whole~~
like sunbursts of egg yolk
swallowed whole and washed down
with a glass of fire
(then I will spit up the flames
burning down the kitchen
until there is nothing left
but ash and cinders
and family secrets
exposed)
I want to eat Anne Sexton for breakfast, lunch
and dinner, all of her,

the heels, the ~~sadness~~/sorrow, the rouge,
the blue eyes, the cigarettes
and Martinis, the jangly bracelets,
French perfume and (suicide watch?)
the frayed ends
~~and nerves that wore out~~
and moths that died
clinging to her chest
and closet,
I want to love her a little,
grope and nuzzle and drizzle,
~~and if she wants to love me back a little~~
touch/trace the children lost/locked
in her hair and constellations,
call her Annie or Miss or Mother,
and if she wants to love me back a little,
if she wants to eat me in return
(the shaved head, the small magic hands,
blacklung wellwater,
the stillborn mutant wing)
great
but it's not necessary
I need to be the one eating her
so I can become a witch
and ~~succubus~~ she-wolf and gravity-babe
and dirty my clean silver spade
(by moonlight?)
~~in someone else's cold cold grave~~
in someone else's cold and remote grave

twilight lay with a dead writer?
dirty dirty spade?
palsied natal wing?
small magic hands
or small tragic hands?
children lost
in her locks and constellations?
witch's hair and its constellations?

(Photo of Anne Sexton torn from the book *A Self-Portrait in Letters*, taped into Piers's Journal)

Contrasting the checked sunfrost
of her strapless bathing suit
and the ground upon which
her chair rests (elements fashioned as
twins by the camera's celestial overexposure)
Anne, lounging, dark moviestar sunglasses,
bare limbs like toasted stalks,
regal languor to the incline of her head,
reminding one of a Queen in repose.
She could be Cleopatra on Valium,
calmly awaiting the tragic destiny of asp.
She could be Jackie O. sunbathing in Greece,

far far away from a slow-motion drive in Dallas.
She could be Anne Sexton
having escaped herself
in a postcard dispatched from Cairo or Capri
or Shangri-La, a cursory note
scrawled in haste—
Having a great time without you,
Love, Anne

The novelty of a stable, normalish life wore off. Piers grew bored and the boredom grew claws and tore at her insides.

Then, one evening, she found a remedy, a palliative diversion of sorts, when Teresa came into Red's with her family. Tall mustachioed father, rotund mother, two young brothers who could have been, and perhaps were, twins, and Teresa, who Piers hadn't seen in over two months. Her short dark hair was now streaked flamingo-pink and she was wearing a neon-green tube-top that corseted her upperbody like an erotic bandage.

Piers, who was in the kitchen, held the favorable position of being able to see Teresa who couldn't see her, and throughout dinner Piers alternated her gaze between the back of Teresa's head and her summer-browned shoulders. She greedily snapped mental photos of her, a scrapbook set to burn.

Piers expected to remain the silent, invisible voyeur, yet when Teresa and her family got up to leave, Piers hustled out of the kitchen and called out—Hey Teresa.

Teresa and her father turned around, nearly in sync, and the rest of her family's heads followed suit.

One of the brothers pointed—Hey, that's the girl who does the puppet shows!

He waved vigorously, as if to a celebrity.

Piers waved back.

Teresa waved too, yet her wave was slight and infirm, her voice strangely flat—

Hey there.

Can I talk to you, Piers said, and Teresa turned to her dad and told him she'd be in the car in a minute.

Her father hesitated, looking at his daughter, then at Piers. Teresa's mother looked at her husband. The brothers fought over the Gameboy they were attempting to share.

After Teresa's family left, the two girls shared a brief,

awkward embrace, followed by a casual exchange, in which Piers mentioned Teresa's flamingo-pink streaks and Teresa mentioned the fact that Piers's hair had grown in and that she had pierced her labret (silver stud with black onyx setting). And when Teresa, her voice wet with hurt, said to Piers *where have you been*, Piers, in wanting to minimize or eliminate the sense of rejection she knew Teresa was carrying in her chest and head, went into a long and elaborate fiction about her *disappearance*, which had nothing to do with Teresa and if she wanted to hang out...

From that point forward Piers and Teresa hung out nearly every night, getting drunk and stoned and completing each other in various ways.

An adverbially inflamed Teresa fell hard for Piers and loved her swoonfully, piningly, achingly, loinfully, gaspingly, inviolably, subhumanly, deep-seedingly, couldn't get enough of her, told her things like *you enable me to breathe*, and considered Piers her soulmate, the one whose rogue independence she would draw from to gather the strength and courage neededto ditch Redline and head out into the great wide world.

Piers, on the other hand, was not in love with Teresa, not in that way, but she enjoyed her company and friendship and the way she gave her body and holy fire without reserve, she enjoyed reading Teresa Anne Sexton poems and enjoyed Teresa's sensually tubercular responses to Sexton's words, as if she were swallowing tiny drops of razored rain, and she definitely and deeply enjoyed the banshee-pitched, convulsive reactions that surged from Teresa when she was being eaten out.

You might say: Piers was on the periphery, playing at love, while Teresa was seriously and thickly in the middle of it.

Gwen saw the changes in Piers, who in the first month of having lived with her had been sober, who would now come home smelling of weed and alcohol. This saddened and frustrated Gwen, made her want to shake sense into the young girl (who Gwen still believed was twenty-one) but she didn't say anything about it, yet Piers sensed her disapproval, and grew inwardly irate—she's not my fucking mother—and then defaulted into sneaky-evasive mode and began coming home after she knew Gwen had gone to sleep, avoiding the silent searchlight of her judgment.

Piers and Gwen had developed a rapport and would discuss many things—Henry's rapidly deteriorating health and what they could do for him, the customers at Red's, (Gwen affectionately lampooned them through spot-on impressions that cracked Piers up,) movies and books, (Gwen loved thrillers and mysteries and Stephen King novels,) Gwen's concern about her son getting shipped off to the Middle East, traveling fantasies, etc., but the topic of Pier's indulgences had never entered their conversations.

Which was why Piers was completely taken by surprise when, one afternoon, the two of them were sunbathing in the backyard and Gwen asked her if she needed professional help.

Piers raised her sunglasses and looked at Gwen—Professional help? Like how? For what?

For substance abuse, Gwen responded point-blankly. There are programs, treatment centers, things like that. There's help.

Piers suddenly felt as if she had been written into an after-school special, and a triumphant ending was only several moral lessons away.

It was the first time anyone had ever mentioned the possibility of treatment in regards to her vices. Insult, shame, outrage, and confusion, blended choppily together, and took her stomach for a spin.

She reasoned to herself—I'm only seventeen and I need to use up all my youth and I'll naturally outgrow certain behaviors—but what she said to Gwen, making sure to smile when saying it: I don't need treatment Gwen. Maybe an exorcist but not treatment.

Henry and Piers sat in Elizabeth and looked up at the stars.

It was a clear and warm summer night.

Henry said he would miss nights like these, tolling the gong of a man whose words were already from beyond the grave.

In a relatively short and brutal span of time, he had grown gaunt and emaciated, bearing the blanched look of a serial insomniac. He had lost his hair, (he and Piers now shared a style, with Piers having gone back to her shaved-head look as a show of solidarity, referring to her and Henry as the Two Baldies,) and he struggled with breathing, chest pain, nausea, and a death's claw assortment of aches and ailments.

Henry knew it was only a matter of time before he had to quit his job at Wal-Mart, which would potentially mean loss of his medical coverage. Pinched in the crossbones of a Catch-22, Henry, during a recent hospital stay, had quipped to Piers—You can go broke dying. And if you manage to live, you'll be in debt until the day you die.

Piers leaned back and indicated a glacial wink of a star—Isn't it crazy that what we're seeing is already dead?

How do you mean?

I mean the stars we're seeing burned out billions of years ago, they're not really there, they're ghosts. The entire night sky is filled with ghosts. I think that proves this is a haunted universe, don't you?

A haunted universe. Sounds about right.

Henry started coughing and kept coughing and then spit pinkened saliva over the side of the boat.

Seems I got a ghost in my lungs, Henry wheezed.

Maybe you swallowed a star.

Yea that's probably it. Too much starstuff in my diet.

Another siege of coughing wracked Henry's body. Piers placed her hand on his back and kept it there.

She and Henry had been coming out to Elizabeth regularly. Sometimes Piers would get stoned beforehand, and one time she had brought a couple of joints with her and asked Henry if he cared to partake and Henry, who hadn't smoked weed in over twenty years said, what the hell, and for the first and only time Piers and Henry got stoned together.

On that occasion Henry had told Piers about the letter he had written to the I Love Gwendolyn Parker Fan Club, the one he had never sent and had never told anyone about, she was the first, and he should probably give the letter to Gwen, she'd probably get a kick out of it, didn't Piers think that she'd get a kick out of it, and suddenly the boy recessed cave-deep inside Henry came to light, beaming through his eyes and voice, the fourteen-year-old boy who had a magnificent crush on Gwendolyn Parker, a.k.a., Elizabeth Starling, or perhaps vice-versa, it was that Henry, nervous, uncertain, awkward, rose-flush with vulnerability, who said to Piers—You've been living with Gwen, has she ever, has she ever said anything that made you think she might like me *like that?*

Henry's fragile assertion of boyhood instantly turned Piers into a mother, *his* mother. Her voice, bright and solid, an umbilical anchor, was not her own, it was a voice belonging to the source from which all mothers found the right and lasting words—I don't know if she feels that way, Henry. She may, but if not, I do know she thinks a great deal of you.

Henry nodded. Piers went quiet.

Thirty seconds later the spell wore off.

Henry was once again fifty-three-year-old Henry, Piers was seventeen-year-old Piers, and that was the one who asked Henry the question that caught him off-guard—Henry when you first took me in, did you think you were gonna fuck me? Is that what you hoped for?

Piers's words came to Henry either too fast or on delay, and in either case blurred.

What did you say?

Piers, who had blurted the question without forethought, replayed the echo of what she had asked, felt self-consciousness creep in and softened her voice—I was just wondering what you thought of me.

Well—Henry started then paused, allowing the rest of his words to catch up and arrange themselves in the right order—I thought you were, you seemed like a lost kid who needed help. That's how I thought of you. And I wanted to help you.

Piers mused on the term *lost kid* before asking—Did you think of me as a lost boy? Or as a lost girl?

I don't know, I guess a girl. Yea, a girl, but mostly I saw you as a kid, a lost kid.

Piers nodded. Henry went quiet.

When they started talking again they had moved on to a different subject.

Henry's hacking fit finally came to an end.

I need a smoke, he said and withdrew a Winston from its pack, lit up, managed a series of short staccato puffs (the longer deeper inhalations demanded too much of his lungs), and spoke what had sort of become his gallows' catchphrase every time he smoked a cigarette—I'm fighting fire with fire.

Piers shook her head and smiled. She didn't tell Henry how she had classified his action as right-wrong.

Despite having replaced the mysteriously vanished Joe with a new Joe, DeLeon had not been inclined to send Joe #2 and Max #2 after Piers. Instead, he did his best to put her out of his mind and tried to willfully disregard the fact that she had robbed him blind and gotten away with it: no consequences, no repercussions.

Between running the club, dealing, shooting short films, parenting, and laboring to write the latest incarnation of his screenplay, *Exit Strategy*, DeLeon stayed busy. Then, in August, several factors aligned in altering his course in bringing him face-to-face with Piers.

His younger sister, June, was getting married, and she had asked him if he would give her away (seeing as he was her older brother, her *only* brother, and their father was dead). DeLeon, motivated by love and devotion to his sister, (and also by self-serving interest—the feds had made Tabanid a target of surveillance, so it was the perfect time to close the club for three weeks for renovations,) told his sister he would be at the wedding, which was in Dallas.

DeLeon, who had a fear of flying, rented a green Chevy Impala. Compelled by his subconscious, a compass with mercenary intent, he chose a route which would take him through Redline, not really expecting that Piers would be there, but since he was going that way it wouldn't hurt to take a look-see. So on the night of August 14th, DeLeon checked in at the Land's Inn and after eating dinner decided to cruise around town.

He drove slowly and stared out the window with listless curiosity, and at 9:23pm, DeLeon's subconscious rose to meet the possibility that life is a scripted and designed affair, when he saw Piers bopstepping along the side of the road, listening to her Walkman.

His hand instantly tightened around the steering wheel.

There she was, walking alone, the little rat who had stolen from him, who he had watched steal from him again and again and again, courtesy of the tape from the security camera.

DeLeon drove even more slowly, allowing Piers to gain distance, then he worried that if he drove too slowly it might seem suspicious and draw her attention, so he accelerated, but only slightly.

He watched as she extended her arm and skated her fingers along the top of the fence to her immediate left and then turn the corner.

DeLeon idled in neutral, 4-5-6-7, and then drove around the corner and followed her trajectory as she crossed through a parking lot. The lot, which was closed, was devoid of cars, yet as an open space that was illuminated on two corners by street-lamps, it wouldn't have been the best place to. . . it was then that DeLeon realized he wasn't sure what he was going to do to Piers. Encountering her had seemed such a remote and far-fetched notion that he had not given proper preparatory thought to *what-if.* When he had sent Joe and Max after her, there had been a plan, a strategy. And now?

DeLeon parked his car on a street adjacent to the parking lot.

He opened his glove compartment and took out his .38.

He got out of the car and began following Piers on foot.

After cutting through the parking lot, DeLeon looked right and saw Piers walking down a narrow side street, populated by maybe a dozen houses. He continued following her, maintaining measured distance.

The block, in conjunction with the horizontal street cutting across its far end, formed a T, and beyond the T lay a side entrance to a park.

Piers jaunted along an inclining path and where it leveled off she could go either right or left.

She chose left and then walked a paved path that curled past a baseball field with bleachers to the right, stately trees and a grassy field beyond the trees to the left, and she walked until she reached a box-shaped playground and stopped at its perimeter.

DeLeon froze. Did she know she was being followed?

He ducked behind a tree.

He felt foolish, as if he were involved in some kid's game which he was too old to be playing.

He glanced out from behind the tree.

Piers was now perched on a swing, thrusting her legs forward and kicking them back, generating momentum.

DeLeon couldn't believe his luck. He felt that the script was advancing in his favor, that its progression justified his actions, or his actions in the making.

He moved along the grass banking the outer perimeter of the playground, until he was directly in line with the swing on which Piers was swinging, a distance of about twenty feet between them.

Piers, who had gotten stoned with Teresa about fifteen minutes before DeLeon had spotted her, was oblivious to everything except the music coming out of her headphones and the sensation of swinging.

DeLeon approached slowly, cautiously.

He wasn't sure what he was going to do until he was doing it: right hand seizing the chain-link just above Piers's right hand and derailing her forward arc movement. Piers whelped what-the-fuck as the left half of her body jerked from the swing, left hand clutching at air, left knee scuffing against the blacktop while her right hand clutched the chain-link, her right foot hooking the edge of the swing and the momentum caused her to corkscrew about 120° before she let go and spilled hard onto the blacktop, now facing the direction from which the sabotage had come.

She saw the pink eyes and the whitefeather eyebrows, the pale face and the leather hat. She saw the gun. It was the first time she had ever had a gun pointed directly at her face. All she could do was blink.

DeLeon wanted to say something clever, something movie-like, but no words came. Even though she was lying on the ground, less than a foot between them, a part of him still hadn't fully registered the reality of the situation: he had her, the thief, the dirty little thief. And now he had to decide what he was going to do with her.

DeLeon and Piers remained silent, the only sound between them the music still coming out of Piers's headphones.

Shut that off, DeLeon ordered, needing to hear words come out of his mouth.

Piers clicked off the Walkman.

Stand up, DeLeon commanded.

Piers used the chain-link for leverage in hoisting herself to her feet.

It was then, with Piers fully standing, that DeLeon realized just how small she was. He knew that she was short and slight, but to see her after not having seen her months, except for on video-tape or those times when she infiltrated his dreams (in which she always seemed and/or felt bigger), and now he was confronted with the immediate reality of a young girl, a child really, like Zoe, (*not like Zoe*, his brain snappishly amended, she was not like Zoe, they were different,) but still, she was just a messed-up kid.

Piers, sensing a shift in DeLeon, what qualified as an opening, a possibility, a chance for survival, said—Please don't kill me. My father is dying and he needs me. Please don't take me away from him, not now.

DeLeon stared at Piers.

Just a messed-up kid, but still *something* had to be done.

DeLeon slapped her across the face, once, hard.

And Piers began crying.

She so badly didn't want to cry, but there was nothing she

could do to stop it. The tears poured forth, and because they were coming from her eyes and not her hands, she couldn't enclose them in a fist or dam them with her nails,

her eyes cried, a bloodletting of tears.

She cried and she shook and then she dropped to her knees and kept on shaking, an animal healing itself through shivers.

DeLeon could feel the fuzzy heat from her face still clinging to his palm. He shook his hand several times. He looked down at her—What you did was wrong. You stole something that didn't belong to you.

Piers remained far gone in her fit of sobbing.

DeLeon thought he heard her blather *I'm sorry* but he wasn't sure, maybe it was just what he wanted to hear and so that's what he heard.

It's done between us, he said and turned to walk away.

That was when Piers scuttled along the blacktop until she reached DeLeon and clutched the bottom of his left leg while sinking her teeth into his calf with rabid intent.

DeLeon tried to shake her off but couldn't. He shook and shook and Piers's head and neck violently jerked back and forth, but she remained pitbullishly clamped to DeLeon's calf.

DeLeon, seeing no other alternative, took aim at the back of her head, and just before he was about to pull the trigger, he changed his mind and used his free leg to stomp on the back of Piers's leg, specifically targeting the calf. Tit for tat.

Piers yelped like a scalded dog and relented her lockjaw, rolling onto her back.

DeLeon, now employing the bitten leg and he kicked her repeatedly in the ribs, face, and head.

Piers covered her face with her hands and curled up into a ball.

DeLeon scowled—Consider yourself very, very lucky because

I was going to shoot you in the back of the head.

Fucking rat, DeLeon spit on Piers, and then left.

Piers slowly counted to nine and then let out a scream.

Gwen:

She walked in and I was shocked. The whole right side of her face was a mess. Swollen and bruised and there was a gash under her right eye, and above the right eye there was a lump like a purple Easter egg. When I asked her what had happened, who had done this to her, she said it didn't matter, it was something connected to L.A. and it was over now. I told her I was gonna call the police, but she begged me not to and repeated that it was over. She said she didn't want to talk about it or think about it anymore.

So I gave her medical attention and looked at her face and got angry, so angry I was shaking. . . I remembered this time my son had come home from school, he must have been around eight or nine, and he had a black eye and a split lip, and when I asked him what had happened he said that a boy, older and bigger than he was, had beaten him up for some stupid reason that I can't even remember. Looking at my son's bruises, I felt heartsick, but thinking about the boy who had done this to him, the boy who was older and bigger, *that* sent me into a rage. . . looking at Piers, I kind of felt the same.

And honestly, I think I was a little angry with her, too. For her stubbornness, for not telling me more, for. . . I don't know what else for. But I held her for a while and she let me. That was what we needed, the both of us.

last night
anne sexton
visited me in my dream
in a livingroom
that was anne's livingroom
(so was i visiting her?)
she was wearing a fringed shawl
her voice was husky/sort of smokerubbed
speaking nearly in tongues
hands flying everywhere
like she was conducting bees
like conduits to full blown mania
i tried to take it all in
tried to digest
didn't say a word couldn't say a word
anne's monologue hoarded the airspace
disjointed run of words words words
and then specific words parceled out
(how it felt: *specific words parceled out*)
anne's eyes/voice pleading, warning—
don't be afraid to speak your dark
those afraid to speak their dark die alone
because dark spoken fuses with light
and dark unspoken is consumed by more dark
next thing i know
we're in anne's backyard
she's sunbathing and getting red real quick
like timelapse sunburn
and i'm splashing around in an inflatable kiddie
pool
watching her get burned but not feeling worried
or concerned or anything

Piers's Journal, August 23rd, 1990

I want to eat
Anne Sexton for breakfast
like toxic cereal
like bacon fat
like sunbursts of egg yolk
swallowed whole and washed down
with a glass of fire
(then I will spit up the flames
burning down the kitchen
until there is nothing left
but ash and cinders
and family secrets
exposed)
I want to eat
Anne Sexton for breakfast,
lunch and dinner, all of her,
the heels, the sorrow, the rouge,
the blue eyes, the cigarettes
and Martinis, the jangly bracelets,
French perfume, and suicide watch,
the frayed ends
and moths that died
clinging to her chest
and closet,
I want to love her a little,
grope and nuzzle and drizzle,
trace the children lost

in her locks and constellations,
call her Annie or Miss or Mother,
and if she wants to love me back a little,
if she wants to eat me in return
(the shaved head, the small magic hands,
the taste of wellwater,
the stillborn mutant wing)
great
but it's not necessary
I need to be the one eating her
so I can become a witch
and she-wolf and gravity-babe
and dirty my clean silver spade
by moonlight
in someone else's
cold and remote grave.

"Even in the pink crib
the somehow deficient,
the somehow maimed,
are thought to have
a special pipeline to the mystical,
the faint smell of the occult,
a large ear on the God-horn"
—Anne Sexton, "One-Eye, Two-Eyes, Three-Eyes"

Note: The large ear on the God-horn reminds me of what Seldom
Ran used to tell Rea about the Universe having the biggest ears

and lots of them and they are always tuning in, always, <u>always</u>. And I wonder: do the pipelines to the mystical get clotted, gummed, jammed, etc., cuz of all the Shit in the World, all the pollutants & toxins that fuck up our clarity?

I say Yes.

Universe with the Big Ears, did you hear me?

Yes, yes, yes.

Piers's Journal, August 30th, 1990

Henry is now staying with me and Gwen. He had been getting around with a cane but more and more he's using a wheelchair and he needs looking after.

At first he hated the wheelchair, said it made him feel like an invalid, but I've become his "pusher" and take him out for spins and try to make it fun for him, and I think he's getting used to it and maybe even enjoying it a little.

Henry's oncologist was happy when Gwen said she was taking him in, but he also reminded her that if things got to be too much, hospice care was an option. Gwen knew hospice care was not an option for Henry, who didn't want to spend the last chapter of his life in Albuquerque, (where the hospice was) and she assured the oncologist that Henry had people to take care of him. By people she meant me and her, which I guess made us Henry's family. And Jacques too.

Henry requested that we do an All Through the Years marathon, which I'd never seen, and though Gwen was embarrassed, she agreed, and so on Sunday we watched all 18 episodes of the first season, (the only season in which Gwen appeared) and it was strange to see the young pretty blonde on the screen who also happened to be Gwen. Something 14 yr old Henry had written in his letter struck me as poignantly right-on and accurate. He had written— *You can feel Elizabeth's heart. It comes through. And in feeling Elizabeth's heart I can feel my own.*

After Henry went to sleep, (he is now in the bedroom I was in and I'm on the couch) I told Gwen about the letter, and she was surprised and touched and then I asked her if she was in love with anyone, and she said she wasn't and she hadn't been in a long time.

After Gwen went to bed, I lay awake thinking how Gwen loved Henry the same as she loved all her customers at the diner, they were family to her, and I guess she loves me like that too.

14 yr old Henry was right and wrong about Elizabeth Starling: You could feel her heart come through, but it wasn't Elizabeth's heart you were feeling, it was Gwen's.

Piers's Journal, September 9th, 1990

Henry doesn't get out of bed much anymore. He listens to his John McCormack records all day long. He is also talking less and eating less. When he does talk, it's in this soft sluggish monotone, like his words are attending a funeral or something.

The other day he told me he wished his father was more patient with him, would give him more time, as if his father were still alive, and then he practically repeated the same thing but in the past tense. He floats in and out of timelines. Sometimes it is winter outside and he is excited to go out and build a snow fort with his best friend Jake. Sometimes it *was* winter, and he remembers building snow forts with his best friend Jake and how he misses it. On one occasion he mistook me for Jake and asked me about the treasure map I'd hidden and when were we going to take off on our big adventure. I told him soon and he was happy.

Sometimes I don't know how to respond to the things Henry says or asks me, and I don't. I just do like Jacques, who is pretty much in Henry's room 24/7, and sit there and look at him.

He likes for me to read to him and told me what his favorite books were when he was younger, I found some of them at Lucy's: "Treasure Island", "Robinson Crusoe", "Robin Hood", and "King Arthur and the Knights of the Round Table". He tells me that as a boy he didn't like reading so much as he liked being read to. The sound of the words coming from someone else's voice made the words feel realer or truer.

This morning when I was reading him a passage about Lancelot's love for Guinevere, he suddenly sat upright and squeezed my forearm—I don't want to be forgotten. I know I'm nobody special, but I don't want to be forgotten.

I could see the terror in his eyes and feel it in the way he was gripping my arm.

I promised him that he wouldn't be forgotten.

He let go of my arm and patted my hand and told me I was good, that I was a beautiful boy with wings.

He also confessed that he had read some of my journals when I was in the badlands. He said they had been left out on the kitchen table, like some kind of invitation and he wasn't sure if that's what I intended but he had read them, and he was sorry for what had happened to me. He said a child shouldn't have to go through that and he kept saying sorry like he was the one who had done something to me, like he was the one who needed to be forgiven. I kept nodding and not saying anything, and then again he told me I was good and beautiful boy with wings and it felt like a gutpunch, and I had trouble breathing.

After he fell asleep I inspected my arm in the mirror. There was nothing there, not a single mark to indicate growth or signs of transformation. Even though it looked and felt the same as it had prior to the freeze and mutation, I knew it was different, or I was different. I just didn't know how.

I'm mooring my rowboat
at the dock of the island called God.
The dock is made in the shape of a fish
and there are many different boats moored
at many different docks.
"It's okay," I say to myself,
with blisters that broke and healed
and broke and healed—
saving themselves over and over.
And salt sticking to my face and arms like
a glue-skin pocked with grains of tapioca.
I empty myself from the wooden boat
and onto the flesh of the Island.
—Anne Sexton, "The Rowing Endeth"

Henry died on Sunday, September 16th in the late afternoon.

Gwen was at work.

Piers and Jacques were with him.

Piers had been reading to him about King Arthur and the Knights of the Round Table questing for the Holy Grail when Henry's breathing grew choppy and irregular. Piers enclosed his hand in hers and repeated his name several times. There was a flinty heaving followed by a phlegmatic rattling.

It sounded as if Henry were drowning.

Piers squeezed his hand tighter, and what came to mind was how she and Trink had been wreckmates, and she said to Henry, as if flinging a desperate confession—Me and you are wreckmates, Henry, we're wreckmates.

Henry's breathing suddenly evened out, a purring respite before a final death rattle, and then he was gone.

Piers looked down at Henry's bluish face, at the eye patch covering his right eye. She had never seen Henry without the eye patch, had never seen what lay beneath, and briefly considered removing it but then felt that it would be a violation of his dignity.

Piers hadn't been with her Aunt Sylvia when she had died. When she saw her aunt in the casket at the funeral, surrounded by flowers and cards, perfectly ordered in her elegant white dress, Piers had the same feeling she was now having about Henry, that the whole thing was a gag or prank, that Henry was playing dead, that the sickness, like the ensuing death, hinged on the dramatic arc, connected to the role he was playing, and now that a climax had been reached. Any second now, any second, Henry would break from character and open his eyes and rise up and say

Let's go to Red's for chow, or Wanna pay a visit to Elizabeth?

Stop playing dead, Piers thought to herself, and this thought burrowed deep and burned, and then she spoke the scalded words aloud—Stop playing dead—and she got pissed at Henry when he didn't stir or acknowledge her words. When he didn't quit play-acting, Piers let go of his hand and left the bedroom and went into the living room where she stood and looked down at her hands for a long dry spell.

That night there was a thunderstorm.

Gwen was asleep in her bedroom and Piers, who was wearing the yellow raincoat, was curled up under a blanket on the couch, violently shaking.

When her heart couldn't take it anymore, she got up and went to Gwen's bedroom.

She quietly opened the door and softly called out—Gwen.

No response.

She made her way toward the bed and took off the raincoat and laid it on the floor.

In a T-shirt and boxers and socks, she climbed into bed and crawled under the blankets.

Drawn by the warmth coming off Gwen's body, she sidled up against her.

Piers was scared that Gwen would turn away and take the warmth with her, but she didn't.

Without opening her eyes, Gwen slid her arm under Piers's neck and shoulders and cradled her head.

Piers, encouraged by Gwen's gesture, drew her knees tight to her stomach and laid her head on Gwen's chest. She flattened her cheek against Gwen's breast and rested her hand just above Gwen's navel.

Gwen could feel Piers trembling.

She pulled her in close and allowed her forearm to curl around the side of Piers's head as her fingers delicately and rhythmically brushed the edge of her hairline, a tactile lullaby.

This she did until Piers stopped shaking.
Soon they were both asleep.

Gwen:

It was about two weeks after Henry died. I got home from work and found a letter on the table, and next to the letter there was a small red gem. The letter was pretty short. She thanked me for everything and said she wasn't sure where she was heading next, she was thinking Key West or maybe Brooklyn, where she knew some people, or maybe Prague, if she could raise money for a plane ticket. She told me the gem was a red onyx and that it had come from one of the Golem's eyes. She wanted me to have it because onyx was powerful and was supposed to help with grief and negative emotions. And she said she had put a patch over the Golem's onyxless eye and now she calls him Henry (smiles).

That was pretty much it. Oh, and there was the drawing at the bottom of the letter... You wanna see it?
(Gwen leaves the kitchen and returns with the letter.
She unfolds it and indicates
a pencil drawing of Piers
holding a balloon which reads
We Love Gwendolyn Parker)

Yes, I know, it was very touching and very sweet. I wish I could have said goodbye to her, but I guess she wanted to leave on her own terms. Anyway, she said she would write, and who knows, maybe one day she'll come back to visit.

Teresa:

Yea it was kind of fucked up. No, not kind of fucked up, it *was* fucked up, the way she just left without saying a word to me. I heard about it from Gwen. I hadn't seen or heard from Piers in like, two weeks, and I went to see Gwen at the diner and she told me that Piers had taken off and had left her a letter. At least Gwen got a letter. So yea, I was pissed *and* heartbroken.

We had made all kinds of plans and talked about things we were gonna do together... my dad had bought me a Polaroid camera for my birthday and me and her took tons of photos, and she had this great idea for a project, it was gonna be called the Polaroid Variations, and we'd dress up as different famous people and stage different scenes... like, for instance, there was one we did called Fireproof Joan of Arc and Piers was Joan of Arc and in the picture she's shirtless and facing backwards so you can see her angelwings, and she's holding a fire extinguisher in one hand and a big glass of water in the other. We were gonna do a whole series—Joan of Arc, David Bowie, Calamity Jane, Amelia Earhart, Marilyn Monroe—it was gonna be this epic scrapbook, ya know, *our thing.*

You know what's really interesting and kind of disturbing? One of the last photos I took of Piers was this one:

Piers standing at the mouth
of the industrial tube
i.e. "the tunnel" at the ditch
wearing a cowboy hat
righthand flashing a peace sign
lefthand pointing an orange water pistol
Kill Your Idols T-shirt
w/ blowup headshot
of crucified Jesus
torn beige carpenter pants
purple Docs
thumbprint of light
bleaching the far upper right corner
of the photo

You see how it looks like she might've just gotten out of the tunnel? Well actually, it was the reverse. Just after I snapped this photo she sort of glided backwards, and when I went up there she wasn't in the tunnel, and when I walked through it I couldn't find her on the other side. I kept calling her name Piers, Piers, Piers, Piers… nothing, and after like twenty minutes, I started to freak out. And once I stopped looking and stopped calling out her name, she popped out from behind a tree and said Tada, and scared the shit out of me. I asked where she had gone, really what I should have asked her was *why* she had gone, and she said, I remember her exact words, she said *Why Teresa, I vanished into thin air. It's one of my special talents,* and she said it in this English accent.

She disappeared for fake and then she disappeared for real.

I guess fall is the perfect season for heartbreak, huh?

Piers's Journal, Undated

For Henry:

The sea is the sea
but it is also a sound recording of the sea.
It is Memory, shroud and fathomless
and freighted with echoes.

Love, Your Wreckmate, Piers

P.S.

This is my tale which I have told
if it be sweet, if it be not sweet,
take somewhere else and let some return to me.
This story ends with me still rowing.
—Anne Sexton

Pierangela Grace Lucener is born to Jean Kelly Lucener on November 27th, 1972, 12:03pm, at the Mercy Clinic in Sunset Hills, Missouri.

She is born feet and knees first, a breech baby.

The fetus that would have been Piers's sister died in utero twelve weeks into the pregnancy and was reabsorbed into her mother's body and into Piers's placenta.

Jean, though having experienced vaginal bleeding in the first trimester, had no idea that she had lost a child. Nor had her doctor been aware of the "vanished twin".

Piers enters the world wailing and marked.

There is a reddish-blue welt, several inches in diameter, which appears on the underside of her left arm. It is covered in what looks like stubby silver filaments.

The obstetrician runs tests and assures Jean that her daughter is fine and that there's no cause for concern. It's a minor and benign aberration that will clear up on its own. Several days later, it is gone.

What the doctor couldn't see, couldn't know, was the length and latency of this shadow, the ghostprint of a wing enfolding many lives in a single body.

About the Author

Originally from Brooklyn, New York, author, poet, playwright and spoken word performer, John Biscello, has called Taos, New Mexico home since 2001. He is the author of the novels, Broken Land, a Brooklyn Tale, and Raking the Dust, and a collection of stories, Freeze Tag. Broken Land was named Underground Book Reviews 2014 Book of the Year.

About the Press

Unsolicited Press was founded in 2012 and is based in Portland, Oregon. The team works to produce artistic and phenomenal fiction, poetry, and nonfiction. Learn more at www.unsolicitedpress.com.

www.ingramcontent.com/pod-product-compliance
Lightning Source LLC
Chambersburg PA
CBHW071128180726
48291CB00007B/2096